"Molly, you know I want you to marry me! And you know damn well why I can't ask you to. What do you want me to say?"

Lady Molly could not meet his eyes. "I suppose to say that you love me."

He tightened his grasp on her shoulders. "That's not right, Molly. You shouldn't want to hear those words from anyone but your dashing Sir Marius."

He dared not raise his voice, but he shook her violently. Lady Molly, balancing precariously on her skates, fell against him. He pulled her into his arms and kissed her. "Now will you tell that fool you won't marry him?"

Books by
Katherine Talbot

Philippa
Theodosia
Lady Molly

Published by
WARNER BOOKS

Lady Molly

Katherine Talbot

WARNER BOOKS

A Warner Communications Company

WARNER BOOKS EDITION

Cover Art by Walter Popp

Warner Books, Inc.,
666 Fifth Avenue
New York, N.Y. 10103

 A Warner Communications Company

Printed in the United States of America

First Printing: April, 1983

10 9 8 7 6 5 4 3 2 1

Lady Molly

No guidebook to the stately homes of England should fail to include Seekings Castle. Uglier than Chatsworth or Woburn, older than Blenheim or Belvoir, Seekings is a monstrous monument to the business acumen of the British aristocracy. Home of the Drayton family since the time of the Crusades, Seekings has grown with each generation.

Ever since Piers Drayton, Gentleman, returned from the Fourth Crusade with two saddlebags of mysteriously acquired gold and the firm friendship of King Richard, the same king who was later to be dubbed Coeur-de-Lion, the Draytons have been known for their wealth. Quietly amassed through centuries of careful husbandry and investments, the Drayton wealth weathered England's economic troubles of the thirteenth and fourteenth centuries unimpaired. The Draytons did not make the mistake of pursuing titles; they were content with the barony that Coeur-de-Lion had given his friend and drinking companion. As a consequence, the Draytons survived the Wars of the Roses. Eschewing matrimonial alliances with the impecunious and warring Plantagenet dynasty, the Draytons refused to emerge from their country fastness to follow the banners of either Lancaster or York.

But when Henry Tudor wrestled the crown of England from the last of the Plantagenets at Bosworth Field, a hotheaded young Drayton fought beside him. When this younger son fell heir to his father's dignities, the King, more concerned with his adherent's wealth than with his valor, raised him from a baron to the Earl of Chettam. The first earl's son inherited his father's impulsive nature, and when the younger Henry Tudor, who had dubbed the second earl a marquis in a fit of amiability after the diplomatic triumph at the Field of the Cloth of Gold, declared himself the Supreme Head of the Church of England, the Marquis of Chettam embraced the reformed religion with ardor. His heirs did not falter from the Protestant path during the dark days of Mary's reign, and his grandson was rewarded with a dukedom by Elizabeth herself.

In Gloriana's reign, the Draytons flourished. Lord Henry Drayton sailed with Drake to the New World; Lady Elizabeth Drayton capped Latin rhymes with her godmother the Queen, who gave her an earl for a husband. The Duchess of Chettam, who had been born a Sidney, had literary tastes and was honoured with an ode by Ben Jonson, as well as by countless less-talented *protégés*. And the Duke of Chettam, blessed with a superb leg and a merry wit, danced with the Queen at Hampton Court and Whitehall.

Yet, despite their frivolity, the Draytons were careful. The Duke danced with the Queen, but he would not accept a post on her Privy Council. "I was not born to affairs of state," he told Her Majesty.

Elizabeth chided him, but gently. "You are a duke," she said, her bright eyes glittering. "Does that not destine you for affairs of moment and power?"

"Your Majesty," the Duke of Chettam replied, bowing very low, "it is because I am a duke that I am able to live as I would wish. *Cur valle permutem Sabina divitias operosiores?*"

The Queen's frown lifted when the Duke enrolled Horace to argue his point. *"Responsare cupidinibus contemnere honores fortis et in se ipso totus teres atque rotundus,"* she answered, dismissing him with a gesture of one bejewelled hand. The Duke hastened home, where, with his daughter's aid, he determined that the Queen had complimented him on his abjuration of partisan politics. His descendents were told his story, and they followed his example, remaining comfortably ensconced in their Sabine retreat at Seekings.

They ensured, however, that Seekings was not the humble farmhouse envisioned by the Roman poet. The second duke built a west wing against the old stone towers and central keep. The third duke's construction of a new court to be laid out according to the precepts of Inigo Jones was interrupted by the outbreak of the Great Rebellion, but he did have time, before mustering his men to serve his king, to supervise the planting of a quincunx that followed Sir Thomas Browne's guidelines precisely. During the Protectorate, the third duke skulked at home at Seekings, nominally under house arrest, but he made the best of the interval by translating Boethius and investing in the latest commercial ventures to India. He did not live to see the Restoration, and his new court was never finished. Instead, his son commissioned Sir John Vanbrugh to construct a fountain court along the east front and a grand ballroom to the south. This became the lesser ballroom when the fourth duchess, a lavish hostess, enveigled her husband into adding a grand ballroom to the west wing.

The fifth duke put a folly on top of the little hill to the east of the castle and had his grounds extensively landscaped by "Capability" Brown. The interior of the castle altered little during his tenure, except for the addition of several hundred pieces of French marquetry and cabinetwork that his foreign bride brought with her from Versailles. The sixth duke left no memorial at Seekings; he died before siring an heir, and his sorrowing widow was displaced by his scapegrace younger brother, who had been sent to India under a cloud of scandal and had infuriated the polite world by returning with a fortune. The seventh duke, a bluff, hearty gentleman, contented himself with renovating the plumbing and heating of the castle, making it as comfortable as a building of its antiquity and size could be. While the eighth duke was said to resemble his flighty French grandmother more than his own stolid parents, he praised his father's name every winter, when the wind whipped round Seekings in search of any crevice through which it could enter and chill the inhabitants. He added the forcing houses—generally admitted to be the finest in Hampshire—to Seekings, saying that he wished for no greater memorial than flowers.

"And strawberries, and beans, and cucumbers?" his younger daughter would ask, and he would always give her the same gentle smile.

The eighth Duke of Chettam was very fond of this daughter, the youngest of his three children, and she could always make him smile.

The Duke was most susceptible to his daughter's blandishments in the evening, however, when his nightly glass of cognac had mellowed his occasionally biting temper, and it was accordingly after dinner that Lady Molly requested a private interview with him to gain his consent to an amateur theatrical production at Seekings.

The Duke granted her interview and even poured out a glass of brandy for her. At twenty-three, Lady Molly was no longer *jeune fille,* and—though of course she could drink nothing stronger than champagne in company—he saw no reason why she shouldn't learn to appreciate fine cognac.

Lady Molly noted with pleasure this sign of her father's good humour, but she hardly tasted her drink as she pleaded her case. Her father reclined in his easy chair, one foot propped on the fireguard, watching her. She sat on the very edge of the sofa, leaning forward to emphasise her statements. The chestnut curls that not even her skilful abigail could make stay up for an entire evening fell becomingly about her face as she put forward all the reasons why, without amateur theatricals, Christmas at Seekings would be deadly dull. Her father did not immediately respond when she had finished. Impatient, she rose and walked over to one of the bookshelves that lined the dark room.

She chose a book and flipped through the pages. The Duke regarded her in silence. Lady Molly's sister, Juliana, was the beauty of the family; both Juliana and Lord St. Omar, the heir, were fair and fine-boned like their father. Lady Molly was quite as tall as her father, but she had inherited none of his indolent economy of motion.

Goaded by the suspense, she turned round after only a few minutes. "You don't need to tell me Aunt Amelia won't approve," she threw at her father, "because she said she would give us her blessing if you would."

"I have no doubt of that," said the Duke. His sister Amelia had kept house for him—nominally, since the servants were far more capable than Lady Amelia Drayton—since his wife's death, a dozen years before. "Amelia seldom questions my decisions. Although I might have thought she'd have Evangelical scruples on this issue."

"To be honest, so might I have thought, Father," said Lady Molly, replacing the book on the shelf. "I had prepared for a tearful scene and was quite overset when she embraced the scheme. Apparently your mother once had a Colman drama staged here?"

"And that was enough to convince Amelia of the propriety of amateur theatricals? I remember the drama— a most tedious affair. I can't imagine why Mama did such a thing, but since she did have theatricals, one would think she could have chosen something better than Colman!"

Lady Molly laughed. She picked up her abandoned glass of brandy and perched on the arm of the sofa. "Actually, I don't think Grandmama's example was what weighed in Aunt Amelia's mind. It was the flattering attentions she received from Lord Alvanley during the rehearsals, I believe."

"Lord, yes, I remember that," said the Duke. "She was *aux anges* for weeks. Nothing ever came of it, of course. And, Molly, she was roundly scolded by our mother for driving out with Alvanley unchaperoned!"

Lady Molly's eyes danced. "Aunt Amelia! I don't believe it! To think of her being naughty! Was it naughty in the last century to drive out unchaperoned, or was my grandmother simply particular?"

"Oh, no, it was most improper," the Duke assured her. "You don't know how lucky you are to be living in the modern age, Molly!"

"I should say so! Such fustian!" Lady Molly agreed, draining her glass. "But you haven't given your consent yet, dear Father. Now surely you won't refuse! You wouldn't want to be stuffier than Aunt Amelia."

The Duke laughed. "Seriously, Molly," he said, "I have no moral prejudice against amateur theatricals. I think they would help to amuse us during what promises to be a chilly winter. But for you to undertake such a project alone—don't you think it will be too much work? With Sir Marius coming, as well."

"Don't you see, Father, it will be something to occupy my mind," said Lady Molly. "And I do so want Sir Marius to enjoy Christmas at Seekings!"

Her *fiancé,* returning from the West Indies after an absence of several years, was to spend the winter at Seekings Castle.

"And I do hope we can assemble an agreeable party,"

the Duke continued. "Will you be able to find a cast of actors?"

"Father, how can you ask that? You know Juliana is splendid, and you must remember Jamie in *Henry V!*"

"Vaguely," said the Duke. "He postured too much, and Jamie is too slight for the hero of Agincourt. But his enunciation was good. And Juliana was certainly amusing as Lady Teazle at Woburn last year." The Drayton family took theatre very seriously.

"I'll ask Juliana to bring down some people who can help," said Lady Molly. "She's sure to know whom to invite."

"You haven't yet decided on a play, though, I gather?"

"You know how Juliana is. Jamie says he'll act in anything, but Juliana can raise such a fuss. I thought I'd consult her when I go up to London next week. A comedy, of course. More than that I hadn't thought. But may I, Father? It would be so delightful!"

The Duke knew his daughter was nervous at the prospect of her reunion with her *fiancé*. This scheme while likely to prove exhausting for her, would at least occupy her mind, as she said. And the Duke of Chettam was never averse to entertaining; Seekings Castle was famous for its hospitality. The very dull relations who invariably flocked home to the ancestral roof for the Christmas session would be leavened by Lady Rich's presence this year—her husband's absence on a diplomatic mission had freed her from Christmas with her in-laws, whom she disliked—but the Duke knew that even Lady Rich's presence could not enliven a house filled with his Fancot cousins and the Dowager Duchess of Wellburn.

"Very well, Molly," he said. "You have my permission. And tell Juliana that she has *carte blanche* to invite whom she likes. She should send a list down here and Amelia will write up the formal invitations. And I shall, I think, invite that charming lady we met in Ravenna last year."

"And her husband?" Lady Molly asked daringly.

"But of course. Now run off and gloat, you absurd child. By the way, Molly, are you to act in this production?"

"No, no. My hands will be full enough with the arrangements for the production."

"And with Sir Marius."

Lady Molly kissed her father on the cheek. "Who knows?" she said. "Sir Marius may be the least of my worries. Thank you, Father."

As she left the room, her father called after her, "And, Molly, do be careful in your selection of a script! So much can depend on that."

"A lovely idea, Molly, my dear, but I give you fair warning that if it's Shakespeare I shan't even attend," drawled the Countess of Rich. "Have another chocolate."

"No, thank you, Juliana. But why do you feel so strongly about Shakespeare?" asked Lady Molly.

Lady Rich squeezed three chocolates before she found one hard enough to suit her. She lifted it into her mouth and then licked her fingers before answering her sister. They were alone, of course, or the exquisite Countess would not have permitted herself such a breach of manners.

"Shakespeare's so dull, and so long. And the women always have to dress as men, which, I assure you, I do not enjoy."

As Lady Molly had no intention of selecting one of Shakespeare's plays, she accepted Lady Rich's admonition with equanimity. "Since I hope you will undertake the role of the heroine in whatever play I choose, Juliana, I will eliminate Shakespeare. Now, have you any suggestions?"

"You *do* want me for the heroine, Molly? You hadn't said so." Lady Rich, whose talent at amateur theatricals was renowned, gave a little sigh of contentment and wriggled into a more comfortable position on her chaise longue. Lady Molly, who detested chaises longues, watched Lady Rich in amazement as she chose her fifth chocolate.

"As I'm to be the heroine, it can't be an historical play," Lady Rich pronounced. "I don't like fancy dress."

Lady Molly, having had long experience of her sister's vagaries, knew better than to speak. Lady Rich selected still another chocolate, while Lady Molly rose and walked to the window. There she looked down at Grosvenor Square for some moments in silence. They were in the boudoir at Rich House, a white and gold room that delicately complemented Lady Rich's beauty—as, indeed, did the rest of Rich House. A tall, narrow building with ill-designed rooms, Rich House could never be wholly satisfactory, but all the *ton* agreed that the present Countess had done wonders with it. The Earl of Rich, it was true, did not seem to appreciate his elegant residence— he spent little time in England—but there were hundreds of other gentlemen happy for an invitation to Rich House, where the charming Countess held a weekly "At Home." While Lady Molly thought her sister's furnishing too *précieux* (delicacy was admirable enough, but chairs that one was frightened to sit on was absurd), few agreed with Lady Molly.

There was nothing to see in the square, as a cold rain had begun to fall, and Lady Molly was happy to turn away from the window when, at last, Lady Rich spoke.

"And if it's to be modern, it might as well be the best. Do a Templeton Blaine."

Lady Molly had not expected this, although Lady Rich's erratic flashes of genius were proverbial among the *haut monde*. "That's a perfect suggestion! Juliana, I am so grateful! His plays are so amusing—I don't know a soul who doesn't like them."

Lady Rich took such praise as her due. "My husband doesn't," she said calmly. "But almost every soul does. I'm looking forward to the new one. Opening in February, they say."

"Oh, there's to be a new one? How nice! It's been at least three years since the last."

"I'm told there's a new one. I don't know its name. I believe they're rehearsing now. I wonder what it's about."

"They won't have started rehearsing yet, if it's not to open till February," Lady Molly absentmindedly corrected. "Juliana, what a splendid idea! I *am* grateful."

"Yes, it is a good idea. I've never heard of any of his plays being given an amateur production."

Lady Molly paced the room, her long, purposeful stride out of place in the cluttered chamber. "Sir Marius escorted me to one. *A Modern Benedick,* I think. Was that playing that year?"

"That would have been *The Unnecessary Duel.*"

"Sorry, that's right. Where the husband fights the wrong gentleman, while his wife elopes with an actor."

"And the songs in the intervals!" said Lady Rich. "They do much to set Blaine apart from the rest."

"Except that one can never hear the words properly on stage. And I'm sure they're clever. That will be an advantage of the Seekings Castle production!"

"You are decided, then?"

"Yes, I think it's splendid. If I can obtain a script. Now, which one should we do? Have you any preference?"

"Do you want to choose now? Perhaps you should wait until you can consult the others?"

"What others? It would be tremendously difficult to decide once all the the guests are assembled at Seekings."

"I wasn't thinking of all the guests," said Lady Rich. "But I thought perhaps you should consult Sir Marius."

"But we can't be sure when he'll return."

"True, there is that. But don't you think he'll want to act in your play?"

"Do you know, I hadn't even thought of it! Sir Marius is sure to insist. I know he's fond of the theatre, and he's often written to me of the theatrical performances on the island. I was just thinking of this as a pleasant way to pass the Christmas season, make a month at Seekings less tedious—I forgot that he himself might enjoy assuming a role."

"I'm sure he will, from what I remember of Sir Marius."

"And I shall be so glad of an occupation for him! When I think that I don't even know how I am to address him!" Lady Molly sat down in the chair next to Lady Rich's chaise longue and took her sister's hand. "Juliana, I'm frightened," she said. "I haven't seen him for more than four years. I don't know—I'm not sure—how does one speak to one's intended husband?" Lady Molly paused, embarrassed by the intensity of emotion she had revealed. "And don't tell me 'affectionately'!" she admonished her sister.

Lady Rich, who disliked levity, withdrew her hands and sat up straighter.

"Molly, you fret too much. There'll be a natural hesitation consequent on your reunion after so many years, but you needn't refine upon it so. As I recall your dashing Sir Marius, he had lovely manners and will know how to put you quite at your ease."

"Yes, he's never at a loss."

"A most attractive gentleman." Lady Rich bit into another chocolate.

Lady Molly was lost in a daydream for a moment, remembering the handsome young baronet—although he was nearly thirty at the time, Sir Marius Wadman had always looked younger than his age—who had waltzed her out onto the terrace at a ball at Carlton House, and kissed her there, that warm May evening when the air smelled of roses.

Lady Molly, too tall for beauty and without the inborn coquetry of her sister, Juliana, had enjoyed her first season, but she'd had no thoughts of romance until she met Sir Marius. She'd reentered the ballroom through the great French windows—to avoid gossip, Sir Marius waited behind for five minutes—knowing that her life would never be the same. Lady Molly hugged her secret to herself, confiding in no one, but no one who had seen her that evening, sublimely unaware of her disheveled hair and her missing ear-drop, was surprised when, a month later, a notice appeared in the *Morning Post* of the betrothal of the Lady Mary Sophronia Drayton, second daughter of the Duke of Chettam, Seekings Castle, Hampshire, to Sir Marius Wadman, Bart., son of the late Sir Adolphus Wadman, of Plumley, Berkshire.

Sir Marius had done well for himself, said the *ton*. The position he had managed to carve for himself in the best society would be secured by this marriage. Always willing to escort ladies, to oblige a friend, or to gamble till dawn, Sir Marius was well enough liked. He was a friend of the Prince Regent and—a more reliable sign of social acceptance—a member of White's. An amusing rattle, everyone agreed, but his lineage was no more than acceptable and his fortune scarcely genteel. Lady Molly Drayton could have done far better.

But Lady Molly was blissfully happy with her choice, and the Duke could see no grounds for objecting to the marriage. However straitened Sir Marius's resources were, Lady Molly would never want for money. The settlements agreed upon by the Duke's solicitor and Sir Marius were more generous than Sir Marius had dreamed, and he was considerably disappointed when trouble with his own inheritance caused the wedding to be postponed. The tangled business affairs left to Sir Marius by his uncle, a prosperous plantation owner, required Sir Marius to sail to Jamaica.

Lady Molly had cried herself to sleep for weeks after Sir Marius broke the news to her. Her father flatly refused to permit her to marry Sir Marius and accompany him to Jamaica, reminding her that his own brother had died crossing the Atlantic to fight the rebellious colonists forty years before. Lady Molly's contention that ocean travel had been vastly improved in the intervening years was met with the alternate argument that, barely out of the schoolroom, she was too young to leave England. The Duke was ably supported in his refusal by his eldest daughter. Lady Rich was fond of Sir Marius and looked forward to welcoming him into the family circle, but she could not approve of so casual a ceremony as a wedding before Sir Marius sailed would necessarily be. It wouldn't look right, she explained to her father, for Sir Marius to take his eighteen-year-old bride, one of the greatest heiresses in the kingdom, across the ocean within days of their wedding. Far better for the young couple to wait a year or so, until Sir Marius was able to return, and then wed with all the pomp and ceremony Lady Molly's rank demanded. Juliana, who had married the very eligible (if elderly) Earl of Rich a year before, was accepted as the family's social arbiter, and the Duke was impressed by her argument.

Even Sir Marius united with the Duke and Lady Rich to refuse Lady Molly's pleadings. Lady Rich convinced him that Lady Molly would be something of an encumbrance on so long a journey, and assured him that her sister would wait for him. Dazzled by the vision of a wedding in St. George's, Hanover Square on his return, Sir Marius left alone for Jamaica, seven weeks after the day Lady Castlereagh had introduced him to Lady Molly Drayton. He remained in Jamaica for four happy, indolent years.

With an effort, Lady Molly wrenched her thoughts away from the past. "So you see, Juliana, these theatricals should help. I do so want Sir Marius to enjoy his first Christmas at home, and Seekings can be so dismal in the winter, if an agreeable party isn't assembled."

Lady Rich asked who would be at Seekings during the holiday season.

"The Fancots, of course. And Jamie's bringing a few of his friends—Antony Laverham, and Mr. Silverton, I think, although we aren't sure yet if they're coming— and Aunt Amelia's asked Lady Wellburn, poor old thing."

"Oh, no, not really!"

"She was born a Drayton, after all. And since she quarrels with Wellburn's wife, Aunt Amelia thought she'd prefer Seekings to Wellburn Court."

"And she does? She's accepted?"

Lady Molly laughed at the gloom in her sister's voice. "Yes, indeed. So you see why it's particularly important for you to invite some amusing people down."

"I should think so. Where are you going to get the cast for your play?"

"Well, Jamie's friends, and the two Fancot girls, and you and Jamie, of course. And Sir Marius. And that pleasant Italian couple—you know, the Conte di Innamorati and his wife."

"The glorious blonde with a silent husband?"

"Yes, that's right. But we shall need some more people —I gave you *carte blanche.*"

"You'll need a few more women, won't you?" asked Lady Rich. Lady Molly did not blink at her sister's rapid assimilation of the list of names, such lightning calculation was instinctive to one brought up in a ducal household.

"Oh, I forgot Phoebe Townley."

"Arthur Townley's wife? She came out the same year you did, didn't she? Their separation made quite a stir last year."

"Yes, I'm very fond of Phoebe, and I can't help feeling it must be dreadful for her. She never complains, but to be treated with such effrontery! She's gone back to live with her parents, in the depths of Dorset. Can you imagine? Nothing to do all day but give lessons to her younger sisters and help her father catalogue his Greek potsherds!"

"Mr. Townley did behave very badly," said Lady Rich. "But won't Phoebe Townley's presence bring a touch of gloom to the Christmas gaieties?"

"I want our house party to be so amusing that Phoebe will be quite shaken out of the megrims. So do, please, find me some amusing guests!"

"I shall do my best—you're right to come to me."

"And remember to get people who will *act,* Juliana! We could always enrol the Trevors or the Dewhursts if we needed to, but it would be so much pleasanter to have the actors all residing at Seekings."

"I said I would try. And I shall."

"Gracious, you sound just like Alphonse when we plan the week's menus," said Lady Molly.

"Molly, I do not appreciate comparison to a servant," said Lady Rich.

"Now you sound even more like Alphonse! He considers himself an artist, you know. But thank you, Juliana. Templeton Blaine was a splendid suggestion. And I must fly now if I'm to find this Mr. Blaine today. I'll be back in time for dinner, of course."

"You're not going by yourself!" gasped Lady Rich. "And where are you going? Why do you need to see the author?"

"Juliana, I'm not a green girl anymore. I shall take my maid, of course, but there's no need for any other escort in London in broad daylight. And as for where I'm going, I can't rightly say. Wherever I am directed Mr. Blaine lives."

"You can't just call on him like that!"

"Why not?" asked Lady Molly, rising from the chair.

"It's not a social call, after all. Strictly a matter of business. And for *you* to be preaching propriety! Don't be so missish!"

Lady Rich sat up to answer to this accusation. "I'm no such thing! Do as you like, Molly, but I don't understand why you need to see the author. Can't you simply buy copies of his plays at Hatchard's? I'm sure they've been printed up."

"Not the one I want," said Lady Molly, walking to the door. "You see, I told you I want to make this house party memorable."

"So which play are you going to do?"

"Which play?" echoed Lady Molly, her hand on the crystal doorknob. "Why, the new Templeton Blaine. It will have its *première* on Christmas Eve at Seekings."

She blew a kiss to her sister and left the room. One of the few points of resemblance between Lady Molly Drayton and her histrionic elder sister was a shared propensity for dramatic exits.

Chapter Three

Major Patrick Costigan, draining a tankard of gin and lemon, had announced to his friends only minutes before he made the acquaintance of Lady Molly Drayton that a miracle from heaven was what he needed. She did not have the golden tresses and the virtuous simper with which Major Costigan pictured an emissary from God, but it took him very little time to realise that she had come, indeed, in answer to his prayer. A portly gentleman whose countenance still bore traces of his youthful pulchritude, Major Costigan was a celebrity in Drury Lane. He knew all the swells, the linkboys would confide to one another in awestruck tones; he had been a friend of Sheridan and was still occasionally invited to sup with Edmund Kean; he was said to have enjoyed a romantic interlude with Mrs. Siddons long before she became the prima donna of the English stage; the Prince Regent himself—to whom Major Costigan bore a decided resemblance—had once walked the length of St. James's with him. In short, Major

25

Costigan was the greatest theatrical impresario in England, and no small share of his fame was due to his position as manager and agent for the reclusive Mr. Templeton Blaine.

Celebrity does not, however, preclude impecuniosity—indeed, the two most often accompany each other—and all Drury Lane knew that Major Costigan was never more than one step ahead of his creditors. His extravagance being equalled only by his garrulousness, all of Drury Lane could have told Lady Molly that, on the day when she came enquiring after him, his affairs were at very low ebb indeed. But no one put himself so far forward as to tell Lady Molly Drayton anything of the sort when she presented her card at the backstage office of the Theatre Royal at Drury Lane and asked how she could get in touch with Mr. Templeton Blaine. The old man in the office did not look at Lady Molly's card.

"You're wanting Costigan," he replied and, turning away, spat a wad of tobacco on the floor. Lady Molly was daunted by this reception, and her abigail begged her, for the fifth time since they had left Grosvenor Square twenty minutes earlier, to abandon this project.

"Do stop tugging on my sleeve, Slater," said Lady Molly. She leaned forward, over the scarred wood of the half-door that divided the public foyer from the back office. "Can you tell me where I can find this Mr. Costigan?" she said very loudly.

"'E's a major," the old man corrected, "and don't you go forgetting it! 'E won't let you."

"Well, how can I get in touch with Major Costigan? I am Lady Mary Drayton, and I wish to see him on an urgent business matter."

Her title pierced the inattention with which the old man felt it proper to greet visitors. "You're a laydy!" he said incredulously and peered at her card. The gilt edges and the coronet in the upper right-hand corner seemed to confirm this young woman's claim, although the old man was too ill accustomed to the protocol of the aristocracy to deduce, from the strawberry leaves on the coronet, that Lady Molly's father was a duke. After a suitable moment devoted to contemplation of the piece of pasteboard, the old man whirled round and subjected Lady Molly to an intense scrutiny.

This was sufficiently novel to amuse Lady Molly, and she waited patiently while the old man took in the glories of her sable-trimmed pelisse, the ostrich feather on her sable-lined bonnet, and the amazing cleanliness of her attire. Only after the old man expelled his breath in a wordless expression of admiration did Lady Molly repeat her request.

"You just stay right here, my lady," said the old man. "We'll 'ave the Major with you in no time at all. 'E'll be in the King's 'ead across the way, him being a man of 'abits, and it being 'alf-past four." The old man whistled and a lanky boy emerged from the other end of the foyer. "Bert, you just 'op over to the King's 'ead and tell the Major as 'ow 'e's wanted on business by a lady." Bert twisted the left side of his face into a hideous grimace and winked at the old man. "A *real* lady," the old man said severely.

"Perhaps Bert here should take my card over to Major Costigan," suggested Lady Molly. Unlike her abigail, who was bridling with offence at Bert's misapprehension, Lady Molly was enjoying herself. As the old man seemed loath to part with the card she had given him, Lady Molly extracted another from her card case and gave it to Bert. His laborious sounding out of her name could be heard as he left the theatre.

Lady Molly had not long to wait. Major Costigan, on seeing her card, abruptly quitted the tavern, leaving his companions to argue with the drawer over the sixpence due for his gin and lemon. He knew his duty to the aristocracy—and he recognised the name Drayton as that of one of England's most powerful families. Bursting into the theatre, he bowed over Lady Molly's hand in the flourishing manner of the previous century.

"And what may I have the honour of doing for you, Lady Mary?" he asked. "Permit me to show you into my private office." He emitted a throaty chuckle. "I fancy I am not unacquainted with the requirements of ladies. May I procure for you a glass of ratafia?"

Lady Molly declined his offer of a drink but gratefully followed him up a small side stairway to his private office. The old man had stared steadily at her while Bert ran his errand; later, Lady Molly told her brother that it was as if she were an exotic caged animal, sent from China or the Indies (a moment later she was to add that she supposed an unaccompanied and respectable young lady probably was as strange in that locale as a zebra or a camelopard). The private office of Major Costigan proved somewhat less salubrious than the open lobby of the theatre, which was regularly swept out. Lady Molly sat down, so as not to offend her host, but Slater remained disdainfully erect, wrinkling her nose at the mingled odours of tobacco, brandy, and other, less identifiable substances. Lady Molly was no less appalled than her servant by the disorder of Major Costigan's apartment, but she praised the lithograph prints of noted thespians that adorned Major Costigan's walls. The Major, thus flattered, explained to Lady Molly that he was on intimate terms with any famous actor she could name. Lady Molly listened politely for a few minutes, then ruthlessly interrupted Major Costigan's reminiscences.

"Yes, but it is not about an actor that I would like to speak to you. You are, I am told, the person to whom I should address enquiries about Mr. Templeton Blaine."

The Major, lowering his voice as he always did at the mention of his most famous acquaintance, admitted that this was the case. "Although," he added, "I cannot promise that I'll answer such enquiries, Mr. Blaine being a very private person, as they say."

Lady Molly disclaimed any designs on Mr. Blaine's privacy and explained her business. Major Costigan did not let Lady Molly know how timely her arrival was; with all his wasteful ways, Patrick Costigan still prided himself on driving a hard bargain. Lady Molly left the theatre some twenty minutes later, having written out an extremely generous draft on her father's bank. But in her hand she clutched a prize—a prize the fading light prevented her from examining until she alit from the hackney in Grosvenor Square. Lady Molly spent the rest of the afternoon secluded in the bedroom her sister had given her; when she descended to dinner some two hours after her return, she looked very, very pleased with herself.

Lady Molly's triumphant glow did not subside in the coming week. It was eight days after her successful negotiation with Major Costigan that Harry Calver mentioned it to Mr. Oliver Brougham. They were sharing a bowl of rack-punch in Mr. Calver's pleasant bachelor rooms in Half-Moon Street, after an evening's gambling at White's.

"I say, Brougham, d'you know Lady Molly Drayton?" young Calver asked. "I danced with her last night at the Castlereaghs' ball. Dev'lish fine girl."

Mr. Brougham furrowed his brow for a moment. "I don't believe I'm acquainted with her. She's Lady Rich's sister, isn't she?"

"Yes, but she's quite a different style from the fair Juliana."

"If my memory doesn't fail me," warned Mr. Brougham, "she's engaged to Marius Wadman."

"What, that court-card? He's been gone for years—out in the Bermudas or some such place."

"That's the man. Fair hair; pleasant manner; not a penny to bless himself with," Mr. Brougham corroborated.

"Damme, if I were to marry a girl like Molly Drayton, I wouldn't be off in Jamaica," Mr. Calver replied, his indignation making him lose control of his grammar.

Mr. Brougham sighed indulgently. "Is she such a beauty, then?"

"No, not really. She couldn't hold a candle to Juliana Rich. But she's got a way of smiling at you, y'know, as if you were the only man in the room."

Mr. Brougham, who knew Lady Rich's wiles well, said he knew the manner Mr. Calver was talking about. Something dry in his tone caused Mr. Calver to protest.

"No, you don't understand. She was telling me all about how happy she is. And she looked it, I must say."

"She's probably glowing because her *fiancé* is finally returning," Mr. Brougham said unsympathetically. "I heard at the club yesterday that Wadman's coming back."

"She didn't tell me that," said Mr. Calver.

"I thought not."

Mr. Calver was silent for a moment. Fortunately, his infatuations were many, and this was not the first time his fancy had hit on a lady whose heart was already claimed. It would take him a day or two, Mr. Brougham knew, and then he would return to his usual heart-whole way of life. "She was telling me all about her theatrical project. How happy she was that she'd snared a new Templeton Blaine to put on at Seekings over Christmas. You'd think she could have mentioned that she was betrothed," mused Mr. Calver.

Mr. Calver's final, plaintive sentiment was ignored by his interlocutor. "She'd done *what?*" Mr. Brougham thundered at his friend, leaping to his feet.

"Gotten engaged," Mr. Calver obligingly repeated.

"No, dammit, the Templeton Blaine!" Mr. Brougham was pacing up and down the crowded room.

Mr. Calver, bewildered by this sudden ferocity in the soft-spoken Mr. Brougham, patiently explained, "She's bought the script for the new Templeton Blaine. You must have heard a new one is opening in February. Well, they're going to do it first at Seekings Castle, privately. Mind you, the Duke must have paid through the nose for the play; that Blaine fellow can ask whatever he wants."

Mr. Brougham put his hand to his head and pulled at his black curls. He was an alarming sight, striding furiously across the room, kicking out of the way a riding crop and a pair of gloves that happened to be on the floor.

Harry Calver, disconcerted by all of this, continued to speak, more rapidly than before. "It should be a good show. *My* parents'd never permit private theatricals, let alone have my sister arrange it all, but I suppose the Duke of Chettam can do as he likes. Pity I have to be in Northumberland with the family—I'd love to be at Seekings. D'you remember St. Omar, Brougham? He'll be in it, no doubt, and the fair Juliana."

"Quite a family affair, isn't it?" Mr. Brougham said savagely, not ceasing to pace the room.

Even Harry Calver could not miss the scorn in Mr. Brougham's voice. A chivalrous young man, Mr. Calver defended his lady-love's scheme. "Lady Rich'll be good, Brougham. Didn't Byron call her the greatest actress of his acquaintance?"

"Byron, I apprehend, referred to her dealings with Lord Rich, not any professional thespian skills," Mr. Brougham flung over his shoulder.

Mr. Calver laughed uncertainly. Hoping to calm his mysteriously offended guest, he persevered. "But it's the new Templeton Blaine! Such a *coup* for Lady Molly—I understand it was her idea. People will be coming in from four counties to see the production, even if no one in it can act or sing at all. I wish I'd been invited to participate; I might even cry off from going home. All those late hours, *tête-à-têtes* behind the curtains, ladies in those quaint costumes. . . ."

Mr. Brougham broke in to Mr. Calver's reverie with a passable imitation of his usual lazy good humour. "You're thinking of Wycherley or Congreve—Blaine's not nearly that *warm*. And the costumes in the three Blaine plays I've seen are considerably more modest than one of Lady Rich's ballgowns."

"But there's to be a ball, too! What I wouldn't give to be there—even with Sir Marius Wadman round. What I wouldn't give!"

His ingenuous exclamation struck Mr. Brougham. He stared at Mr. Calver for a moment, then lowered himself into an armchair. "Yes," Mr. Brougham murmured, "the house party at Seekings should be most interesting."

With that cryptic utterance, Mr. Brougham relapsed into his customary languid state. He chaffed Mr. Calver on his admiration for Lady Molly Drayton, played a friendly hand of picquet (friendly because Mr. Brougham, a superb card player, refused Mr. Calver's suggestion of guinea points), and drank the better part of a second bowl of rack-punch before taking his leave. Mr. Calvert had forgotten Mr. Brougham's uncharacteristic spasm of energy before the first punch bowl was drained (possessing as he did a happy propensity for putting the incomprehensible out of his mind), but Mr. Brougham preferred to take no chances. His insistence on mixing up a second bowl over the spirit lamp meant that he himself incurred a certain unsteadiness of gait and, the next morning, a nasty headache, but Mr. Brougham was willing to sacrifice his dignity in a good cause.

Unsteady as his gait was when he reached his chambers in the Albany that night, Mr. Brougham was sufficiently sober to remember a task he had set himself. Rooting through the pile of invitations his valet had left on the mantelpiece, tossing dozens onto the floor, Mr. Brougham found a rose-coloured card from the Countess of Rich before he retired to his bed.

Chapter Four

Although Lady Molly would never have admitted it, she envied her sister's way of life. Not all aspects of it—Lady Molly disliked her ineffectual brother-in-law—but Lady Rich's unquestioned position as the most dashing hostess in the _ton_ was appealing. Lady Rich's weekly salon, as Lady Molly knew, was celebrated as the most amusing event of each week in the London season. Mr. Luttrell had written one of his clever rhymes about the glittering company that assembled at South Audley Street; Beau Brummel, before his unfortunate flight to the Continent, had graced Lady Rich's drawing room several times; and, although Lord Rich might grumble at the expense, the champagne his wife served was never less than exquisite. Lady Molly privately thought that dispensing champagne at an afternoon party was absurdly extravagant. Lady Rich cited Mme. de Récamier's example in defence of the practice, but manners were different in London, and, Lady Molly uncharitably reflected, everyone knew that Juliette de Récamier, for all her charm, was not *bon ton*.

Lady Rich's extravagance did make her parties convivial. Juliana prided herself on knowing every new *crim. con.* story before the outraged spouse's action was taken to the courts. Conversation was uninhibited at Lady Rich's (as were actions, occasionally), which explains why Lady Molly was not shocked by her first encounter with Mr. Brougham.

Lady Molly of course knew Mr. Brougham, the nephew and heir of the Earl of Annesley, by repute. Even had he not been one of the fashionable young dandies whose doings were celebrated in all the society journals, Mr. Brougham had been at school and university with Lord St. Omar, who was only a few years his junior. Jamie was still wont to speak with bated breath of Kit Brougham's mountaineering exploits on the college roofs. Lady Molly had noticed the handsome young man with the dishevelled dark curls when he first entered the room. He had glanced round, raised a hand or smiled in greeting to several people and then walked directly over to the sofa where Lady Rich was holding court. Lady Rich dismissed her *beaux* and held a private colloquy with the latecomer for a few minutes. Lady Molly, maintaining a conversation with Mrs. Rawdon Crawley as she watched her sister, concluded that the stranger was her sister's latest flirt. She was pleased, then, and surprised, when Lady Rich brought him over to her. Lady Rich performed a perfunctory explanation, informing Lady Molly that Mr. Brougham had particularly requested to be presented to her. Mrs. Crawley scented an intrigue, her sharp eyes flashing from face to face, but with Lady Rich's hand at her elbow she was forced to float away.

They were left alone, and Lady Molly—who was happy to be relieved of Mrs. Crawley—smiled at her companion. Kit Brougham drew in his breath and began to talk to Lady Molly. He would never be able to remember what he had said to her or she had said to him in those first few minutes; they spoke of nothing that either had not discussed a dozen times before—the weather, the elegant appointments of Lady Rich's drawing room, Mrs. Crawley's scandalous friendship with Lord Steyne, the excellence of the champagne they both were sipping. But then Lady Molly laughed—a low, happy sound—and Kit Brougham abandoned courtesy.

"You are not at all what I expected," he told Lady Molly, interrupting her polite retort to the witticism that had made her laugh.

Lady Molly, disconcerted, asked the obvious question. "What did you expect, Mr. Brougham?"

No other woman, Mr. Brougham reflected, could have asked that without coquetry. This glorious girl with honest grey eyes made it a simple question. "I thought you'd be more like your sister," Mr. Brougham answered, matching her directness.

Lady Molly flushed, remembering Mr. Brougham's apparent intimacy with Juliana. "No, I'm not much like Juliana."

Mr. Brougham heard the note of apology in her voice and was suddenly furiously angry. "Don't talk like that," he said, putting a hand on her arm.

They had been standing to one side of the fireplace, at the far end of the long drawing room, but there were people nearby, and something in Mr. Brougham's expression made Lady Molly pull away from his touch. Mr. Brougham took two steps forward and grasped her arm firmly. Lady Molly, unable to free herself, turned and walked with him to the most isolated corner of the room. Half-hidden by the heavy draperies of the window facing South Audley Street, Mr. Brougham and Lady Molly resumed their conversation with no one to hear.

"You think you should be like Juliana, don't you?" Mr. Brougham asked, still incredulous. He reached out and put his hand high on the wall. Leaning there, he seemed to bar Lady Molly from the rest of the room. When he realised she was not going to answer his question, he spoke again. "That's foolish, my dear. Lady Rich is lovely, of course, but she's far from well liked."

Lady Molly sipped her champagne and found enough courage to meet Mr. Brougham's eye. "I know that," she said. "Juliana never gets along with other women, for one thing."

Mr. Brougham chuckled and persevered. "Even if Lady Rich were Helen of Troy—"

"I've never heard that *she* got along well with other women!"

"You know what I mean. Even if your sister were a pattern-card of all virtues, you shouldn't waste time fretting that you'll never be like her."

"I don't! I mean, even if she were, I wouldn't!"

"No?" Mr. Brougham's eyes did not leave Lady Molly's face.

Blushing, she smiled at him. "Sometimes," she admitted. "But then, don't you envy others sometimes? Envy's a sin we all indulge in, I had thought. Even Shakespeare. How does the sonnet go? '... Wishing me like to one more rich in hope, featured like him, like him with friends possessed, desiring this man's art, and that man's scope. . . .' "

"If the great poet admits doubt, who am I to deny it? Yes, Lady Mary, I confess I have, er, 'troubled deaf heaven with my bootless cries,' but—"

"I am never called Lady Mary!"

Mr. Brougham apologised and, signalling to a footman, obtained a fresh glass of champagne for each of them. Lady Molly noticed that he hadn't bothered to ask whether she wanted a second glass. Accustomed to punctilious courtesy, Lady Molly would ordinarily have disapproved of such high-handedness, but she did love champagne— and Mr. Brougham had recognized her quotation. This conversation was preposterous, she told herself, but nonetheless she waited for Mr. Brougham to finish what he had been saying.

He did not do so until the footman was out of earshot.

"Your case, my dear Lady Molly, is something quite different. It is your sister who frightens you, who makes you so unsure of yourself, who is, I venture to say, ultimately responsible for this ill-conceived betrothal of yours." Mr. Brougham's indignation had led him too far. Lady Molly, who had been uneasy at the beginning of his tirade, was furious when he finished.

"How dare you! We've never met before, yet you seem to think you know me better than my family does— or than I myself do! How, pray, can you condemn my betrothal? You know nothing of its circumstances or of my *fiancé!* You know nothing of me!"

Mr. Brougham looked up from his wineglass, which he had been turning lazily as she spoke; his apparent inattention further infuriated Lady Molly.

"I don't know you very well," he said. "But better than you think. Well enough, anyway."

"Well enough for what?" demanded Lady Molly.

"To know I want to marry you."

Lady Molly's eyes grew very round.

"Drink your champagne," advised Mr. Brougham. "Perhaps not so efficacious a restorative as brandy, but it should serve. Then you can tell me all the reasons why you won't marry me. Although I will make it clear before you do so that I haven't asked you to—I merely expressed a wish."

Lady Molly, mutely obedient, sipped her champagne while Mr. Brougham rattled on. "I haven't asked you to marry me now because—well, my dear, no one likes rejection, and rejection is written all over your incredulous face. But I will ask you, someday when I think I have a fighting chance of gaining an acceptance."

"But I am to marry Sir Marius Wadman!"

"You won't, though. When did you last see him?"

"He sailed for the West Indies in the summer of '15," Lady Molly stammered.

"Month? Day?"

"I'm not sure. June, I think."

"How often does he write to you?"

"Once a month! Usually, that is, I mean."

"I see."

Lady Molly wrenched herself out from this spell. "I don't know why I'm bothering to answer your questions! I cannot imagine why you seem to have succumbed to a sudden passion for me—"

"That's an ungracious way of putting it," Mr. Brougham interrupted. "I have informed you that my intentions are strictly honourable."

"All the same, they are offensive!"

"I don't see why. You can't believe in the emotion you have inspired? You are suspicious of precipitancy? I wonder why. How long had you known Sir Marius before you decided to marry him? I'm acquainted with him, you know, and his methods are famous. I can't imagine you withstood them for long—not at the age of eighteen!"

"How do you know my age?" Lady Molly demanded.

"A chance hit, I see. I thought it had to have been your first season when you were so imprudent as to agree to marry him."

"And what do you mean by his *methods?* How dare you imply . . ." Lady Molly's voice trailed off as she struggled with her rage. "I am perfectly capable of deciding my own future—and I was just as capable four years ago!"

"How long had you known Sir Marius before you thought you were in love with him?" Mr. Brougham persisted.

Lady Molly would have said that she was furious with Mr. Brougham; his tone, his questions, and his astonishing declaration offended every sense of propriety. Yet, she answered his question, meeting his eyes and smiling bravely.

"A week. Or maybe less—I don't remember."

"You see?" said Mr. Brougham. "And I need hardly point out that there are innumerable literary precedents."

Lady Molly raised an eyebrow.

"For love at first sight," Mr. Brougham explained. He smiled. "Your eyebrows are almost black. A pretty contrast to your hair."

Without moving her eyes from his face, Lady Molly said softly, as if to herself, "I cannot believe this conversation."

"You find it difficult to believe someone can fall in love with you? Sir Marius has been sadly remiss."

Mr. Brougham let his arm fall from the wall and straightened himself. Lady Molly realised for the first time how tall he was.

"I'll convince you someday," he said. "Someday soon."

Mr. Brougham bowed slightly and walked away. His final glance was a caress and Lady Molly felt her cheeks burning. She spent ten minutes at her sister's party after Mr. Brougham's departure, but, as soon as she could, she escaped to the solitude of her bedchamber, where she stared at herself in the mirror for a long time.

"What did you talk about with Kit Brougham?" Lady Rich asked her sister that evening. "You were *tête-à-tête* for such a long time! Did you like him?"

Lady Molly was fond of her sister, despite everything, and so answered without hesitation. "No! The most odious man! He behaved as if he'd known me for years!"

Lady Rich wrinkled her pretty brow. "That doesn't sound at all like Kit Brougham. Though I know how unpleasant that sort of familiarity can be."

Lady Molly saw that her sister was laboring under a misapprehension. "Not that sort of familiarity," she assured Lady Rich. "Nothing vulgar or encroaching. He described my character."

"Oh, I see. But that can be rather flattering, my dear. Why didn't you like him?"

"Flattering! I felt like a passage from Horace he'd been set to construe!"

"You like Horace, don't you?" murmured Lady Rich.

Lady Molly laughed and stretched out her legs, closer to the fire. The two sisters had dined out and attended a musical *soirée,* and were now sitting in Lady Rich's boudoir, discussing the events of the day. Lady Molly had not dared mention Kit Brougham, but she felt immensely relieved that Lady Rich had given her the opportunity to express her assessment of his character.

"The arrogance of it!" said Lady Molly. "That's what I can't bear."

"But what did he say?" Lady Rich asked. "I'm dreadfully curious. And do you think he was correct?"

"Of course he wasn't correct! No one could be on a first meeting! Unless . . . Juliana, what had you told him about me?"

"So he wasn't so off target after all!" said Lady Rich, laughing.

Lady Molly glanced at her sister and then gazed into the fire. "He wasn't so wrong," she said with a slight shrug. *"Had* you spoken of me?"

"No, I haven't," Lady Rich said, with the infinitesimal pause she always used to mark her rare sincere statements. "Dearest, why should I be telling a presentable young man about my younger sister?"

Lady Molly laughed. "I just wondered . . ." she said, raising her hands helplessly.

"But now you must tell me what he said. Please, Molly!"

"He said I was too much in awe of you, for one thing!"

"Did he? He's right, you know. You may think you're disapproving—and you're quite uncomfortably censorious—but you're never at ease in my house, and I think it's because you haven't yet learned that you shouldn't try to be in the same style as me."

"I don't try to be in your style!" cried Lady Molly.

"Maybe not consciously, but all the same, in some ways you do." Lady Rich looked at her sister through half-closed eyes. "Your hair, for example. Mine *must* be arranged as high as possible—my height, you know—but you're too tall to have it piled on top of your head."

"You're not suggesting I wear it loose?"

"No—but it's a pity you can't. Your hair's such a lovely colour. Quite elegant."

"What *do* you propose I do with it?" asked Lady Molly, smothering her resentment.

"Looser, definitely. Curls cascading round your shoulders, that sort of thing. You have good shoulders, too. Cécile will know what to do—I'll send her to you tomorrow night."

"Thank you. My hair never *has* stayed up for a full evening!"

"And another thing, Molly. If you don't mind?"

"Go on, Juliana." Lady Molly sighed. "But do leave me some self-esteem."

"I'm not criticising you, darling!"

"True—my shoulders are good, and so is my hair."

"Your hair's only good if you find a new way to arrange it," Lady Rich qualified.

"Yes, Juliana. And what's the other thing?"

"You should never wear white! Much too *ingénue!* And those pearl rosettes on your gown tonight are dreadfully *démodé.*" Lady Rich spent the next quarter of an hour enumerating the changes that ought to be made in Lady Molly's appearance. Lady Molly serenely listened to her sister's strictures. Lady Rich, vastly experienced in the progress of *amours,* had no hesitation in ascribing her sister's unprecedented humility to the impression Kit Brougham had made on her, although Lady Molly had not repeated much of their conversation. Lady Molly would not admit it, but Lady Rich was quite sure that Kit Brougham had admired her. Lady Rich had long deplored her sister's inconvenient sense of propriety and could think of nothing more amusing than to see Lady Molly engage in an *à suivi* flirtation. Lady Molly might protest her dislike of Kit Brougham, but Lady Rich knew better than to believe her sister. Smiling as she discussed Lady Molly's wardrobe. Lady Rich devised a plan.

As for Lady Molly, she could not understand why advice from Juliana had always before been so unwelcome. Juliana's odious condescension didn't hurt anymore, and her counsel on clothes was well worth hearing. Although, Lady Molly told herself comfortably, Juliana was not always right. Lady Molly listened to her sister's advice, evaluating it as she would anyone else's, discarding Juliana's more flamboyant preferences and bowing to her more perceptive observations. Except on her wedding day, Lady Molly would never wear white again.

Lady Molly Drayton could spare no more than a week in London. November had begun, guests were converging on Seekings, and she wanted to start the preparations for her play. She also had to return to Seekings to await the arrival of Sir Marius Wadman.

She had not long to wait. The third day after Lady Molly's return home, as she was in the midst of a conference with the estate carpenter about the platform stage he had been commissioned to build in the lesser ballroom, the butler entered the ballroom (where he gave a most disapproving glance to the lumber the carpenter had already brought in) to announce Sir Marius's arrival. Lady Molly, as might be expected, greeted this information with less than her usual composure. "Oh, dear, and here am I in all this confusion! Where did you put him, Newcome?"

"The morning room, Lady Mary. Tea will be served shortly."

"Thank you for calling me instead of Aunt Amelia! Oh, but I have this odious frock on! Excuse me, Phillips— you can decide the rest on your own, I think. And I'll see that some men are sent in to help you. How did he look, Newcome?"

The butler smiled; Lady Molly was behaving, in his estimation, just as a young lady ought on the unexpected arrival of her betrothed. "If I may say so, Lady Mary, Sir Marius seemed impatient."

"Did he?" Lady Molly's hand went to her hair, which was pulled back in a simple coil at the nape of her neck. "I shall be with him directly. Please see that the blue room is prepared for Sir Marius, Newcome."

"Yes, Lady Mary. May I say, Lady Mary, that I wish you very happy."

Lady Mary thanked Newcome and left the ballroom. Sir Marius had evidently met with Newcome's approval— as she had met him in London, this was his first visit to Seekings—and Lady Molly could not but be gratified to hear that, with disregard for propriety, he had asked to see her alone before being greeted by Lady Amelia. She walked quickly through the three corridors between the lesser ballroom and the morning room and then paused, her hand on the crystal knob of the morning-room door. Realising that her footsteps would have been heard and thus her hesitation was perceptible to the man inside, she bit her lower lip and opened the door.

Sir Marius Wadman rose from the lemon-brocaded chair in which he had seated himself and crossed to where Lady Molly stood. He drew her into the room, closed the door behind her, and took her hands in his.

"My dear," he said, "you haven't changed." She had, of course, but Sir Marius knew better than to say so, even though the change was, for the most part, an improvement.

Lady Molly stared up at Sir Marius. She had forgotten

how handsome he was. Unable to say that, she remarked, "Your skin is so brown."

Sir Marius lifted his head and laughed. He had not released her hands, and now his grasp on them tightened and he drew her closer to him. "It's the sun in Jamaica. No way to avoid it. I look like a farm labourer, don't I?"

Lady Molly had no intention of telling him that his bronze skin and his sun-bleached hair were quite amazingly beautiful, and she thought he might have realised that she knew the sun in the tropics was stronger than in England. She withdrew her hands from his warm clasp.

"Do sit down, Sir Marius, and tell me how you descended on us so unexpectedly! I'm delighted, of course, but I thought you'd write from London."

Sir Marius explained that he'd decided to come straight on to Seekings from Southampton, and added that he hoped she would forgive his impetuosity. "I was persuaded, my dearest, that you would excuse my riding clothes."

Lady Molly stiffened. "Of course. Shall I ring for some tea?"

The coltish girl he had left behind him had had no such grace, Sir Marius reflected, but she would have given him a more enthusiastic welcome.

Lady Molly knew her coolness disappointed Sir Marius, but the excitement that had gripped her before she entered the morning room had quite evaporated when she came face to face with her betrothed. He was a handsome man with an engaging smile and a pleasant voice, but Lady Molly, looking at Sir Marius, could scarcely believe that there had been a time when seeing him across a room would cause her to miss a step in a dance, or that she had once drawn in her breath and broken off her sentence every time a fair-haired man with broad shoulders crossed the pavement in front of her phaeton, or that the red and gold dragons with which the Prince Regent had adorned his ballroom at Carlton House had once seemed beautiful simply because it was under their baleful glance that she had first danced with Sir Marius.

Lady Molly served tea to Sir Marius, and they spent an hour in polite conversation before the Duke, Lord St. Omar, and several of the guests came in from the day's shooting. Lord St. Omar had had a lucky day, and private conversation was impossible while the Duke proudly recounted his heir's triumphs of the day. Some ten minutes after the shooting party's entrance, Lord St. Omar, embarrassed by the encomia he received, managed to inform the Duke that a new guest had arrived. The Duke greeted Sir Marius with his customary courtesy and began to question him about the West Indies. Lady Molly slipped from the room and did not rejoin the company until dinner time.

The following days did nothing to shake off Lady Molly's odd indifference to Sir Marius. She mentally assembled a cast list for her play—the final decisions were to await on the arrival of Lady Rich and her party—and was able calmly to assess Sir Marius's probable thespian abilities. Aunt Amelia remonstrated with Lady Molly for this.

"My dear, I can't help feeling it's not quite *right!* 'Sir Marius hasn't the voice for a romantic hero,' indeed! How *can* you say that, Molly? He's quite how I used to picture Thaddeus of Warsaw, my dear. Such lovely fair hair!"

This revelation of her spinster aunt's youthful daydreams amused Lady Molly. "Can you imagine poor dear Aunt Amelia sighing over Mrs. Porter's romances—and cherishing the image of a Polish revolutionary!" she exclaimed to her friend Mrs. Townley, who replied placidly that Lady Amelia had always seemed to suffer from an excess of sensibility. Lady Molly did not repeat to Mrs. Townley the rest of her aunt's speech.

"There's something improper about it, Molly," Lady

Amelia Drayton had said. "Sir Marius is your affianced husband, and as such you should not speak of him like that!" Lady Molly's protest that she had only meant that his habitual soft, slurred manner of speaking would not carry well on stage was to no avail. "Molly, my dear, I don't know what's wrong with you. One wouldn't think you were to marry Sir Marius in a few months! You show him none of those distinguishing attentions that are expected of a lady to her *fiancé*. Some time alone together is entirely permissible—indeed, expected—and you've hardly spoken to him. And you have always had a free hand with the dinner arrangements—and you're certainly better at working them out than I ever was, my dear— but you really might let him take you in tonight! I watched him last night and the poor man looked quite unhappy. Not that Phoebe Townley's not a charming girl, because she is, but she is not *you,* and Sir Marius is so in love with you, Molly! Juliana's justified in saying you deserve a better match—only a baronetcy, and a recent one at that!—and I wouldn't want to stand in your way, but Sir Marius is very kind, even if he isn't the heir to an earl!"

"Juliana says what? What are you talking about, Aunt Amelia?" demanded Lady Molly, but Lady Amelia folded her innumerable shawls round her, gathered up her embroidery silks and silently drifted away.

Lady Molly stared after her in bewilderment for some moments, then remorsefully assessed her own conduct. While much of Lady Amelia's pronouncement was incomprehensible, it was clear that she deplored Lady Molly's cavalier treatment of Sir Marius. Lady Molly had not, in fact, observed that Sir Marius disliked the place she had given him at the dinner table the night before. Her view had been somewhat impeded by the enormous silver epergne the trustees of the British East India Company had presented to the fourth duke, but it had seemed that Sir Marius flirted alternately wih Phoebe

Townley on his right and Mrs. Fancot on his left throughout the meal. But, whether or not Sir Marius resented her neglect (and Lady Molly was flattered, of course, to think that he might), he was a guest at Seekings Castle and must be treated with propriety. If propriety demanded some show of affection between an affianced couple, Lady Molly knew she must stop avoiding Sir Marius. She let him take her in to dinner that evening, and she sat next to him in the drawing room when the company had reconvened after dinner. She even suggested that Sir Marius might like to accompany her on a ride the next morning; Sir Marius, putting his hand on her arm, readily agreed.

Their ride did little to allay Lady Molly's suspicion that the heady rapture of her first feeling for Sir Marius would never be regained. The day was clear and frosty; all the other gentlemen had gone shooting. Sir Marius professed himself content to join the shoot after luncheon, but Lady Molly felt that he regretted his absence.

Sir Marius, mounted on a skittish black stallion from the Seekings stables, did not appear to advantage. He was an indifferent horseman, and he knew it.

"Shall we ride up to the folly there?" he suggested.

Lady Molly was disappointed at so tame an objective: the folly was no more than a mile and a half away from the castle, set on the far side of terraced walks laid out by "Capability" Brown, at the summit of a gentle rise.

"We shall be returning here for Christmas each year, I suppose," Sir Marius remarked.

"Shall we? Not that I shan't want to, of course, but your relations?"

"I don't have any worth worrying about. You know that, my dear. And certainly none whose hospitality warrants refusing a duke's invitation!"

Lady Molly glanced at him uneasily, but Sir Marius was too occupied with his horse to notice the expression on her face.

"You know, Molly, this play was a grand idea," he continued. I'm proud of you."

Something in his tone set Lady Molly's teeth on edge, but she thanked him for the compliment. They had reached the folly and reined in their horses by this time. When Lady Molly saw that Sir Marius had caught his spur in the stirrup while dismounting, she gave up waiting for his assistance and slid down from her saddle unaided.

"I would have helped you. Why couldn't you wait another minute?" said Sir Marius as he wrenched his foot free, making the horse flinch. Lady Molly gave her reins into Sir Marius's hands and moved to comfort the stallion.

"Touchy prad, that. Quick temper."

Lady Molly did not respond to Sir Marius's entirely unfounded characterisation of the horse, whispering softly in its ear and patting its shuddering sides. Sir Marius hailed an undergardener who was trundling a wheelbarrow filled with dead leaves on the far side of the rise.

"You, boy, come hold our horses!"

"He's working, Sir Marius. Surely we don't need the horses held."

"I want to go inside the folly," Sir Marius insisted. "You should have brought a groom along."

Lady Molly laughed. "You sound like Aunt Amelia. I don't see that it's necessary for a groom to accompany me and my intended husband on a ride in our own grounds, but Aunt Amelia would always prefer me to have a servant along to play propriety."

Sir Marius handed the reins of both horses to the undergardener, who had left his wheelbarrow and scrambled up the hill in obedience to the gentleman's call. "Now, my dear, you aren't thinking *I* want a servant along to play propriety," he said softly.

Lady Molly blushed and walked slowly into the folly.

The folly was charming in the spring and summer, when roses climbed up its seven pillars, but in the winter, with no walls to give shelter from the wind that whipped across the hill, the folly was bleak and cold. Lady Molly shivered, which afforded Sir Marius an excuse to put his arms round her.

His kiss was not unpleasant, but Lady Molly withdrew from his embrace shortly. Sir. Marius caught her chin as she turned her face away. He kissed her cheek and the curve of her neck.

"Have I told you that I think you're beautiful?" he whispered into her hair.

Lady Molly firmly drew away. "It's so cold," she said. "We must go back."

"You've become a proper young lady," said Sir Marius. "But we'll be alone again some other time."

Lady Molly smiled but did not speak. They rode back in silence, Sir Marius well pleased with himself, and Lady Molly realising with horror that she had no longer the slightest inclination to marry Sir Marius Wadman. It was with a sense of inevitability that, entering the morning room after her ride, she recognised Kit Brougham as one of the guests Lady Rich had brought down from London.

Lady Molly drew off her gloves, tossed them onto a table, and, with perfect aplomb, walked forward to greet the new arrivals. She shook hands with Mr. Brougham as if she had known he would be there, Lady Rich thought admiringly. Since Mr. Brougham did not know that Lady Rich had thought it injudicious to inform Lady Molly that he was joining the house party, he could not appreciate Lady Molly's self-command. He could, however, appreciate Lady Molly's beauty. In a close-cut grey riding habit trimmed with French braid, her colour heightened by the wind (and fury at Lady Rich's treachery), Lady Molly was in far better looks than she had been at Lady Rich's party. The golden highlights in her chestnut hair sparkled in the light from the window, and she moved with an easy grace that made every other woman in the room—even Lady Rich—seem squat and awkward. Mr. Brougham, who had been cursing himself ever since the day of Lady Rich's party, was reassured.

Striding home through the London squares that afternoon two weeks before, his champagne-induced elation had subsided; by the time he reached his rooms he was furious with himself, burning with embarrassment when he thought of what he had said to Lady Molly. He had spent much of that day and no small portion of the days following standing at his fireplace, staring moodily into the flames and kicking at the logs with his boot (a habit that drove his batman, whose responsibility the glossy leather was, nearly to distraction). He went over his conversation with Lady Molly again and again, wondering what had possessed him to speak with such insufferable arrogance, wondering why he had felt he knew Lady Molly so well and why he had been so sure that someday he would marry her. Those speculations were pleasant compared to his agonised attempts to guess what Lady Molly must think of him.

So painful were the latter that he almost abandoned his scheme of going to Seekings Castle over Christmas. He had been sure that Lady Rich, if properly approached, would give him an invitation. Before meeting Lady Molly, he had had every intention to be on the scene to laugh at an amateur's efforts to stage the new Templeton Blaine. After meeting Lady Molly, he was more eager to go than ever, but he was curiously reluctant to face Lady Rich; not knowing what Lady Molly had told her. He was unsure how to proceed, changing his mind every hour, until a billet from Lady Rich had summoned him to her side, and she had informed him that she would like him to attend the Christmas festivities at Seekings Castle.

For the second time in a week, Mr. Brougham had stumbled home from Grosvenor Square completely oblivious to his surroundings. He puzzled over the invitation for hours, cudgelling his brains to decide what lay behind it. Had Lady Molly told her sister of his mad declaration? Had that gained him an invitation to Seekings? And his thoughts continually returned to the most important question: what did Lady Molly think of him? When Lady Rich's verbal invitation was followed a few days later by a formal request for his company from Lady Amelia Drayton (Juliana had prevailed upon her aunt to keep the invitation secret from Lady Molly by hinting at an intrigue, which was why Lady Amelia felt so uncomfortable about Lady Molly's treatment of Sir Marius), Mr. Brougham swallowed his amazement and politely penned an acceptance. He wanted very much to see Lady Molly again, if only to prove to himself that the peculiar emotion he had felt was a consequence of drinking champagne in the afternoon. It was one thing to like a girl on first meeting her, or to decide she was a beauty, but no one, Mr. Brougham assured himself, absolutely no one—except in plays—fell in love at first sight. So unsure of this conclusion was he, however, that he spent an evening atoning for his skepticism about Harry Calver's infatuation by permitting Harry to fleece him at cards.

When Lady Molly entered the morning room at Seekings, Mr. Brougham knew beyond a doubt that he loved her, and when she smiled at him he was certain—as certain as he had been that afternoon at Lady Rich's—that someday she would love him. Eager to earn another smile from her, he interrupted her conversation with the Contessa di Innamorati to enquire after the theatrical project. He was rewarded with a warm smile as Lady Molly admitted that she had only been waiting for her sister's arrival before assigning roles and beginning rehearsals.

"But who is to play which part?" "Shall I be in it?" "I hope you don't want me!" "When do you plan the performance?"

All was confusion as a dozen people pressed forward to ask Lady Molly about her play. "Is it true," Lady Wellburn demanded in the stentorian tone of the very deaf, drowning out all other voices, "that this shall be the new Templeton Blaine?"

Everyone else fell silent as Lady Molly turned to where

Lady Wellburn sat. The Dowager Duchess reached for her lorgnette, which was encrusted with diamonds in need of cleaning, and regarded Lady Molly through it. Lady Molly knew a moment's temptation to abandon the whole scheme. Mr. Brougham noticed her sudden pallor and put his hand on her arm. At his touch, she turned and caught his eye for a moment. They exchanged a smile, or the hint of one, before Lady Molly answered Lady Wellburn's question.

"Yes, that's correct, Lady Wellburn. Have you seen any of the earlier plays? The Prince says Mr. Blaine is quite the most amusing man since Sheridan. Now, I do hope you aren't going to say you disapprove of our little plan for the holidays! The Prince has said he might even be able to attend our performance, and I should so dislike to disappoint him."

Lady Wellburn could remember the days when the Prince Regent, now sadly fat and invariably overdressed, had been the finest gentleman in Europe. "Prince Florizel" they had called him then, and, he having had a penchant for women older than himself, Lady Wellburn's name had been linked with his own before it became clear that Mrs. Robinson would be his Perdita. None of the younger people in the room would have dreamed of looking to the boisterous, elderly Prince as a social arbiter, but Lady Wellburn put down her lorgnette and raised a hand to straighten her purple silk turban, smiling as she thought of days gone by.

"Don't be absurd, Mary," she said. "I may call you Mary? If the Prince has given his gracious assent to your delightful little porject, who am I to criticise? In my day, it is true, no lady would have thought of such a scheme."

Lady Wellburn paused and Lady Molly held her breath.

"But that was in the last century," the Dowager Duchess continued. "And this Mr. Blaine's plays are amusing—or so I've heard. The Prince is a fine judge of literature. Mary, if your father doesn't object—and you don't, do you, Chettam?"

The Duke, who had been conversing in an undertone with the Contessa di Innamorati, jumped and looked round wildly for an instant before he located the enormous brocaded armchair where Lady Wellburn was sitting. Lady Molly expelled her breath and began to bite her lower lip. Her father, however, murmured a hasty assent to whatever it was Lady Wellburn had asked him, and the Dowager Duchess finished her sentence. "Then I, my dear child, will simply look forward to your production. What is the name of the play? And what is it about?"

Lady Molly gave her guests a grossly simplified version of the plot. Even simplified, though, *The Procrastinator* was funny enough to make them laugh aloud.

"Only eight actors are needed, then," Lady Molly concluded. "Those who are interested should tell me, so that I may distribute to them copies of the play. Then tonight— after dinner, shall we say?—we can all meet in the rose saloon and I shall decide on the allotment of the parts."

To Lady Molly's surprise, fully half the guests clamoured to be allowed to act in the play; most of the ladies and almost all of the gentlemen. As she had already worked out her cast list, this unlooked-for enthusiasm was unsettling, but she consoled herself that, after all, she still could choose the people she wanted, even if she would have to listen and be very tactful towards the others. The supply of scripts she had commissioned her father's secretary to copy out soon ran out; when Mr. Brougham roused himself from his brown study and sauntered over to request a script, Lady Molly was chagrined to admit that she had no more. Mr. Brougham, though he had not figured in her earlier plans, might well be a notable addition to her cast. Lady Molly seemed to remember that Lord St. Omar had spoken of his thespian achievements at Oxford, and, priding herself on her willingness to be discomfited for the sake of true talent, she had hoped Mr. Brougham would read for her. The two requests for scripts immediately preceding Mr. Brougham's she had dismissed with an airy apology; she stammered as she refused Mr. Brougham.

Mr. Brougham bowed gracefully. "Then Fate denies me entrance to your meeting tonight."

Lady Molly flushed. His tone was ironical; she did not want him to think that she would flatter him with deliberate exclusion.

"Not at all, Mr. Brougham. The doors to the rose saloon will not be barred, I assure you. But if you would prefer to read the play in advance, that can easily be arranged."

She glanced round the room and beckoned to Sir Marius. Mr. Brougham's back stiffened and he held himself very straight as Sir Marius approached.

"May I present Mr. Brougham? Mr. Brougham, Sir Marius Wadman."

"I believe we have met," said Mr. Brougham as they shook hands. "Some years ago, though, I should think. You've been abroad?"

"Yes, I've but recently returned from Jamaica. This will be my first English Christmas since '14."

"I wasn't in England in '14," said Mr. Brougham.

"Paris?" guessed Lady Molly. "Army of Occupation?"

"Quite right, Lady Molly," said Mr. Brougham, cursing himself for his clumsy boastfulness. What did it matter that Sir Marius had sat out the war comfortably in London while he, a romantic twenty-one-year-old, had left Oxford without his degree to fight against the Corsican menace? In another moment he'd be telling Lady Molly about the wound he had received at Waterloo.

Mr. Brougham was disgusted with himself and so, though he had disliked Sir Marius on sight, he forced himself to accept Lady Molly's suggestion that the two of them could work out some way to share Sir Marius's script. Mr. Brougham agreed to come by Sir Marius's chamber before dinner to collect the script.

"I doubt I shall act, but I'd like to read it," Mr. Brougham explained.

"I shan't read the whole thing," Sir Marius admitted, Lady Molly having wandered out of earshot. "She told me she wanted me to read the general's part with particular care, so I shan't bother with the rest."

Mr. Brougham was amused by Sir Marius's lack of interest in the play; he himself thought a new Templeton Blaine worthy of more attention. Sir Marius, with the facile grace that distinguished him, politely conversed with Mr. Brougham about the shooting they might yet get in that day. Mr. Brougham, who was not at all fond of shooting, responded idly to Sir Marius's questions, all the while trying to see what Lady Molly had seen in him.

To his surprise, Mr. Brougham did not feel angry with Sir Marius. He was serenely confident that Lady Molly could never marry this man who wore a lavender-striped waistcoat, whose cheeks were so red, and who could not properly pronounce the word *ptarmigan*. Mr. Brougham listened patiently and indeed almost enjoyed his conversation with Sir Marius.

When Mr. Brougham met Sir Marius before dinner to collect the script, he found himself even more in charity with his rival. Sir Marius offered him a drink and, when Mr. Brougham refused, invited him to sit down and talk for a few minutes anyway.

"It lacks a quarter yet to eight," Sir Marius assured his guest. "And you're dressed."

Mr. Brougham's swallow-tailed coat and knee breeches, while not quite so glossy as Sir Marius's, were impeccably tailored, and his cravat was tied in a *Trône d'Amour*. Less striking than Sir Marius's *Waterfall*, Mr. Brougham's cravat was nonetheless exquisite enough for Sir Marius to exclaim in admiration. Mr. Brougham politely disclaimed any particular skill, not disclosing that he had spent three-quarters of an hour before his glass, perfecting the knot.

Sir Marius gestured Mr. Brougham to a chair. "And what d'you think of this play scheme, Brougham?" he asked. "I heard you crying off this morning. Don't really think it's improper, do you? That's not your reputation."

Mr. Brougham laughed. "I'm not straitlaced, I promise you!"

"But why not the play, then?" asked Sir Marius. "I'm just curious, mind you."

"Annesley—my uncle, that is—wouldn't stand for it, if I may speak frankly," Mr. Brougham explained. "I'd be cut off without a shilling as soon as he heard about the production."

Sir Marius raised the glass of Madeira he had poured for himself from the decanter at his bedside table (these were provided for all the gentlemen visitors to Seekings). "I had an uncle like that, too," he said. "Mine lived in Jamaica, though—not too hard to keep rumour from his ears."

"Mine's eighty-two and, except for gout, is as spry as he ever was," said Mr. Brougham. "He keeps Mr. Secretary Creevey—are you acquainted with him?—writing to him every week. And Creevey knows everything. But I hoped you might tell me something about Jamaica. Your stay there was an extended one, I believe you said?"

"More than four years. Wonderful place, Jamaica. Too hot at times, of course, but a man can live there very comfortably."

"You own a plantation?"

"Yes, and six hundred slaves to work it."

"Mr. Wilberforce's philippics don't trouble you?" Mr. Brougham asked.

"Why should they? Slavery'll never be abolished."

Mr. Brougham, who had suffered his first disagreement with his great-uncle at the age of sixteen, when he had tried to persuade the irascible Earl of Annesley to speak in the House of Lords against the slave trade, and who had spent much money and time in the following ten years seconding Mr. Wilberforce's and Mr. Macaulay's efforts to outlaw the foul practice, did not answer.

Sir Marius seemed a good-natured fellow, and they walked down to the drawing room together on seemingly cordial terms, but Mr. Brougham resolved that Lady Molly, even if she refused him, must not be permitted to marry her *fiancé*.

Chapter Seven

Lady Rich invariably spent an hour of every afternoon in bed, and it was there that Lady Molly sought her, as soon as the gentlemen had departed for the shoot. Ignoring the protestations of Lady Rich's French maid, Lady Molly entered her sister's boudoir and flung open the door to her bedchamber.

"Juliana, are you asleep? Because I want to talk to you."

The mound under the pink satin coverlet shifted slightly. Lady Molly strode to the window, which faced west, and pulled apart the curtains. Lady Rich sat up abruptly.

"Molly, don't! I *hate* the sun in my eyes, and I'm perfectly awake in any case. Though how you dare enter my room when I am resting!"

Lady Molly sat down in the chair nearest her sister's bed. "Does that cream really help your skin? It looks dreadful."

"It should help my skin; it's twenty shillings the ounce. And you wouldn't have to look at it if you hadn't come storming in here."

"I didn't come storming in. And you know quite well why I want to talk to you, Juliana."

"Because I brought Mr. Brougham down without telling you," said Lady Rich with a slight yawn. "Really, Molly, you are too predictable."

Lady Molly was taken aback by this accusation, but rallied fast. "I don't see why you had to keep it a secret, Juliana. Most embarrassing, when I am supposed to be in charge of everyone's accommodations."

"I didn't notice any embarrassment. And Aunt Amelia is responsible for our guests' accommodations, not you."

Lady Molly did not let her sister make her angry. "But you know I do all the work," she replied calmly. "And how did you persuade Aunt Amelia to conceal it from me? I am sure she read me the list of guests."

Lady Rich laughed her celebrated silvery laugh. "I hinted at a romance, Molly dear."

"Between—"

"You and him, of course."

Lady Molly's laugh was almost as artificial as her sister's. "But how absurd! When I am engaged to Sir Marius! Did Aunt Amelia believe you?"

"I rather fancy she thinks you are neglectful of Sir Marius; you know, you didn't write to him as frequently as she thought you should."

Lady Molly had regained her composure, although Lady Rich had noticed nothing amiss. This time, Lady Molly's laugh, was much more convincing. "But, honestly, darling, what could I say if I wrote twice a week? Now tell me, why was all this secrecy so necessary? About Mr. Brougham, I mean."

"Because you never like me bringing my flirts down. I thought you might throw a spanner in the works, as

Jamie says. Telling Aunt Amelia about how wicked I am, you know."

Lady Rich's drawled explanation hurt Lady Molly. She had long suspected her sister of immorality, but hearing that she actually planned to misbehave at Seekings was curiously painful. But, before she could retort, Lady Molly remembered how often Juliana had teased her in the past. Juliana had never had any scruples about lying—and she had not actually said anything more than that Mr. Brougham was one of her flirts. Lady Molly remembered the smile she and Mr. Brougham had shared and was suddenly confident, whatever Juliana might think or say, that Mr. Brougham had come to Seekings to see *her*. Lady Molly was immensely glad that she had not told her sister of Mr. Brougham's astonishing proposal; she could hug that memory to herself while Juliana insinuated the vilest things.

"You do me an injustice," she said. "I would never attempt to say such a thing to Aunt Amelia. Nor can I flatter myself that she would understand!"

"He is very handsome, don't you think, Molly?" said Lady Rich.

Lady Molly did not make the mistake of denying it. "Yes, he's very good-looking."

Lady Rich, disappointed that her sister was not rising to her bait, tried one more cast. "But, then, you prefer fair hair."

Even this did not perturb Lady Molly, although she had forgotten about Sir Marius until that moment. "And hasn't the sun bleached Sir Marius's hair wonderfully?" she said lightly. "Now, Juliana, you must promise never again to spring an unexpected guest on me—particularly one I've told you I dislike—and I will leave you to have your sleep in peace."

"You're not the hostess here. Aunt Amelia is. So don't try to make me feel guilty," Lady Rich said grumpily. "It's almost time to wash this cream off anyway."

"Should I call Elise on my way out?"

"Yes, and tell her to bring the Serkis rouge," said Lady Rich.

Lady Molly raised an eyebrow, but Juliana couldn't shock her anymore. "I'll do that. Will you come down for tea? I'll see you then."

Lady Molly left her sister's bedroom, conveyed the message to Elise (who had lingered suspiciously close to her mistress's bedroom door), and returned to her own sitting room. Lady Molly was oddly happy; she hummed a tune from Templeton Blaine's *The Unnecessary Duel* under her breath as she walked down the corridor.

Although Lady Rich duly descended to tea two hours later, her skin dewy and her cheeks delicately stained with pink, she did not see her sister. Lady Molly found the rearrangement of her *dramatis personae* occasioned by Mr. Brougham's arrival so absorbing that she sent a servant down to ask her aunt to excuse her from tea. Sir Marius was perfect as the general, and Lord St. Omar was ideally suited for the young fop who sought, unsuccessfully, to marry the general's daughter. Phoebe Townley could play the duenna who won the young fop for herself, while Juliana, of course, was to be the *ingénue*.

That left the hero to be cast, the elegant young man who never accomplished anything because he put everything off until tomorrow. The procrastinator of the title, the hero of the play, was a charming young man whom the general's daughter loved despite his fatal disability. Lady Molly felt that of all the guests at Seekings, Mr. Brougham was the one best suited to play the *rôle*.

She had some qualms about casting Mr. Brougham opposite her sister, but she firmly squelched them. Either he had a *tendre* for Lady Rich or he did not, and no amount of rehearsing together could change that. And, in any case, it could hardly matter less to her. Lady Molly turned her mind to the smaller parts, but decided against making any decision about them until she heard people read after dinner. After all, she couldn't be sure who would accept which parts, even if she could make a fair guess as to who would be best in each. There might, she reflected, be a few surprises.

It was Mr. Brougham, characteristically, who provided the greatest of those surprises.

He joined the assemblage in the rose saloon after dinner, but when Lady Molly asked him to read for her, he politely declined.

"I am afraid, Lady Molly, that I cannot accord it with my conscience to appear in a theatrical performance."

Lady Molly stared at him in disbelief.

"Now don't tell me you've seen the error of your ways since Oxford," Lord St. Omar called out.

Mr. Brougham explained, as he had done earlier to Sir Marius, that it was not his principles but those of his elderly uncle which precluded him from joining the cast.

"I deeply regret my inability," he concluded, "and am willing to assist Lady Molly in any aspect of the production short of treading the boards."

Lady Molly was badly disappointed, but Mr. Brougham's excuse was unassailable. One could hardly press Mr. Brougham to go against his Evangelical uncle's wishes. Lady Molly assured Mr. Brougham that she would find some humble task for him to perform.

There were a few other surprises for Lady Molly that evening, but none could rival the one Mr. Brougham had dealt her. The Contessa di Innamorati, it transpired, could make even Templeton Blaine's sparkling dialogue sound like a sermon, but she was so decorative that Lady Molly decided to retain her as the opulent widow whom the general tries to woo. Phoebe Townley, on the other hand, was far better at her part than Lady Molly had expected, flirting with Lord St. Omar with the utmost skill. At half-past eleven, Lady Molly announced her casting decisions.

Mr. Brougham's defection meant that Sir Marius, after

all, had to play the hero, but St. Omar's friend Laverham made a grand burlesque general with whom Lady Molly was satisfied. Her casting of the Contessa di Innamorati proved a master stroke, because several of the gentlemen whom she had passed over insisted that they be permitted to assist the production in whatever lowly position she might find for them. Lady Molly correctly ascribed this circumstance to the Contessa's charm. On the whole, she was very pleased. Her disappointment over Mr. Brougham's withdrawal was short-lived, since it meant she would not have to direct him in those compromising scenes with Lady Rich—courting trouble, after all—and he made it evident that he intended to stay close by her side as she worked on the production.

He had stayed close by her side throughout the evening, laughing at young Laverham's antics, hissing, "You'd think a lady with her reputation would be a better actress," in Lady Molly's ear as they listened to the Contessa di Innamorati orate, and taking her aside at the end of the evening when she took her party to see what would be their theatre.

The huge ballroom was lit only by the handful of candles Lady Molly and her guests had brought in with them. The outline of the half-completed stage could be distinguished at the far end of the room, and the group walked forward to examine it. Several of them had never seen the lesser ballroom at Seekings and were overwhelmed by its size, while the more knowledgeable assured them that this room was far smaller than the grand ballroom.

Mr. Brougham—who was among the uninitiated, but who had seen many such ballrooms—drew Lady Molly quietly aside.

"They won't miss you," he said. Neither of them held a candle, but Lady Molly knew the room well. They walked through the shadows to the curtained window embrasures at the opposite end of the room from the stage.

Mr. Brougham was not accurate in his prediction: Lord St. Omar did notice his sister's disappearance. He wondered what had happened to her, but he asked no one. In her absence, the guests were his responsibility; he herded them all out of the dark room and escorted them back to the drawing room, where the rest of the party were playing cards. Lady Molly was not aware of his efforts on her behalf until the great double doors shut behind the last of the guests and the last glimmer of candlelight was extinguished.

Lady Molly forgot the impropriety of her situation in her curiosity about Mr. Brougham's behaviour.

"Why won't you act in my play?" she hissed, almost before they were out of earshot of the others.

"I told you why, Lady Molly," Mr. Brougham whispered in her ear. "It is on quite a different subject I would like to address you."

"I beg your pardon?"

"Surely you haven't forgotten our earlier conversation?"

"Well, no, but . . ."

Mr. Brougham pulled one of the heavy curtains forward so that Lady Molly could step into the window embrasure. She stepped in, he followed her, and the curtain fell behind them. This was Mr. Brougham's first view of the south terrace of Seekings Castle, and he exclaimed in wonder. The night was dark, so that the topiaried trees, the quincunx, and the home wood beyond were indistinguishable black masses, but the ornamental water shone with the reflected light from the innumerable windows of the castle.

"It is lovely, isn't it? This is my favorite of the gardens. Most people prefer the west terrace, which slopes down, but I like this."

"Can we go outside?" asked Mr. Brougham, fiddling with the latch on the French windows.

"Tonight! Mr. Brougham, it's November! Far too

cold! Look at how the wind whips the water. And neither of us have wraps."

She had answered him instinctively, without a moment's hesitation, as she might her brother. It was only when Mr. Brougham turned away from the enchanted view and took her hand that she realized she should not be there, let alone go walking in the gardens with this man who was practically a stranger. Yet, she could hardly pull her hand out of his grasp and run from the room; she had come willingly enough. His next words did something to reassure her. Though retaining her hand, he spoke in a matter-of-fact voice and made no effort to come closer to her.

"So now that you've seen Sir Marius again, what do you think?"

"What do I think?" Lady Molly could only echo.

"About him," explained Mr. Brougham, with more impatience than passion in his voice.

"He's not the way I remembered."

"No. You were very young. What are you going to do?"

Mr. Brougham was careful not to tell her to break her engagement, nor to tell her not to do so. He wanted to hear what she would say.

He almost got the answer he wanted. Lady Molly, who had been staring off into the looming shadow at the end of the gardens that was the home wood, repeated after him, "What shall I do about Sir Marius? Why, I suppose—"

Here Mr. Brougham tightened his grasp on her hand. Lady Molly broke off her sentence and turned to look at him.

"What do you want me to say? That I won't marry him—that I'll marry you instead? I don't understand at all. Juliana says she brought you down to—how shall I put it?—keep her company. Did you plan this seduction with her?"

Lady Molly's speech had begun in a tone of bewilderment; by the end she had flogged herself to genuine anger. She pulled away from Mr. Brougham.

"Wait. Don't go."

Mr. Brougham was almost as angry as she was. "Can you really believe that? What a high opinion you have of your sister! And of me. Why did you come here with me? I thought you trusted me."

Lady Molly's anger vanished. "I'm sorry," she said, touching his arm with her hand. "I don't understand anything, that's all. And you must admit your behaviour has been most extraordinary."

"Only with you," murmured Mr. Brougham.

"And you're a friend of Juliana's."

"If I weren't, I'd never have met you."

This was so precisely the right thing to say that Lady Molly's heart melted. "I must go," she said softly. "This is dreadfully improper."

"But are you going to marry him?" asked Mr. Brougham, as he had sworn he wouldn't.

"Don't worry so much," said Lady Molly. "And don't expect my emotions to move with your celerity. This is, as Mr. Blaine has his heroine say, so 'improbably sudden.'"

She kissed him lightly on the cheek and then, astonished by her own temerity, slipped through the curtains and ran from the room. After one vain gesture towards her, Mr. Brougham stood still, listening to her footsteps as he watched the wind whip the water into a thousand jewelled fragments.

Chapter Eight

"No, no, pause before entering the room! And look round it first. You are not sure if Arabella is there or not!"

Sir Marius walked back to the empty space where Lady Molly had promised her cast a door would soon stand. He said, "Knock, knock," took a step forward, paused and looked round the enormous ballroom. Then he saw Lady Rich, who was crouching behind an Oriental screen.

" 'Pop rep., Miss Arabella, not half an hour since you swore you loved me! Pretty behaviour!" he declared.

Lady Rich fluttered out from behind the screen and threw herself on Sir Marius's chest.

"I thought you were my father," she trilled in his ear, standing on tiptoe to entwine her arm round his neck. Before Sir Marius could utter his next line, Lady Molly interrupted.

71

"That was much better," she said, walking forward. "But we'll have to move the screen to the left."

"Then I won't be able to see her," said Sir Marius.

"Yes, but the audience will," said Lady Molly. "That's all that matters. I don't think we need rehearse the rest of this scene; you two are already so good!"

"I should say they are too good," the Contessa di Innamorati said to Mr. Brougham, who happened to be sitting beside her in the chairs set out for the audience.

He turned sharply. "Contessa, you think . . . ?"

"I think nothing." The Contessa shrugged her shoulders.

"But you said . . . ?"

The Contessa looked over towards the stage. "If I were the lady, I would not choose to have my *promised* husband in a love scene with Lady Rich," she said with lazy malice.

Mr. Brougham also looked at the stage, where Lady Molly was reading to Sir Marius and Lady Rich some notes she had taken. "I had not noticed," he said softly. "Nor has she."

It was December now. The clear, cold weather of the preceding month had held. The ornamental water was frozen over, but sunlight filled even the far corners of the cavernous ballroom. The three people on the little stage were sharply illuminated.

Lady Rich and Sir Marius, standing side by side, faced Lady Molly. To Mr. Brougham, only a dozen yards away, it seemed as if he were seeing them at a distance, as if he were a spectator looking at a stage far below him in a London theatre. They were superbly posed; the light glinted in Lady Rich's curls, etched Sir Marius's admirable profile against the far wall, and revealed Lady Molly's pallor. The weeks of rehearsal had tired her. Mr. Brougham suddenly felt he must break up this tableau.

He excused himself to the Contessa, threaded his way between the gilt chairs and, disdaining the steps the carpenter had built in, lightly vaulted up onto the stage. Lady Molly gave him a faint smile and pushed some stray curls back from her forehead. Lady Rich caught his eye and, without smiling, moved slightly to indicate that he should stand next to her. Sir Marius, who had lost at cards to Mr. Brougham the night before, made no gesture of greeting but asked him what he wanted.

"I thought you might want to be informed that you'd skipped over eight of your lines in the first scene."

Sir Marius, who naturally did not want to be informed of anything of the sort, glowered at Mr. Brougham.

"Oh, which lines?" said Lady Molly. "I didn't even remark it!"

Mr. Brougham flipped back several pages in the sheaf of papers, sewn together on the left side, that served as his copy of the script. Remaining adamant in his refusal to act, Mr. Brougham had constituted himself as prompter, in which role he had the continual pleasure of embarrassing Sir Marius, who was slow in learning his lines.

Sir Marius was not the only dilatory member of the cast: Tony Laverham invented his own lines for the blustering general as he went through each scene. Lady Molly took this philosophically, admitting that Laverham's lines were usually garbled versions of the original, far wittier ones, but arguing that he was still very amusing. Mr. Brougham found the cavalier treatment Mr. Laverham accorded Templeton Blaine's best lines infuriating. Lady Molly and Mr. Brougham continually wrangled over fidelity to the script; their respect for each other's opinion was evident.

Even in public, where he tried to keep a strict rein on his emotions, Mr. Brougham's enjoyment of Lady Molly's company was plain, as now when she bent her head over his script, her hair brushing his hand as he pointed to the omitted passage. Lady Rich saw the way Mr. Brougham smiled at Lady Molly when she looked up from the script to thank him; Lord St. Omar also saw that intimate smile. Lady Molly's sister and Lady Molly's brother both began to wonder about her.

Lady Molly would have been mortified had she known how revealing that exchange of smiles was; without knowing, she was oddly embarrassed and jumped away to make a general announcement.

"Excuse me, Contessa, Jamie. Could everyone come up here for a minute?"

The Contessa picked up her shawl of Norwich silk and gave it to Lord Dewhurst to arrange round her shoulders. When he had completed this task, the Contessa moved regally towards the stage, Lord Dewhurst and four other gentlemen following her. Lord St. Omar collected the two Misses Fancot from the corner where they had been giggling and brought them up to the stage. When they all were there, Lady Molly began to speak.

"What I thought I'd like to talk to you about, I mean, what I'd like to ask you, is . . ." Lady Molly, in her favorite gesture, pushed her hair back from her forehead, then rapidly finished her sentence. "I wanted to know if anyone had any objection to an extra rehearsal tomorrow. Act two, at three o'clock."

Everyone groaned. "That's what must be expected when we stage the most amusing comedy since Molière," said Lord St. Omar. "We must suffer for art, as Chatterton said."

Lord St. Omar's martyred tone provoked a general laugh, and Lady Molly's demurral went unnoticed. When Mr. Brougham drew Lady Molly down from the stage and led her to a chair, she repeated her statement.

"*The Procrastinator,* much as I love it, is not the most amusing comedy since Molière. Sheridan or Congreve must rank higher."

"I can't agree," said Mr. Brougham.

"No? Why not?"

"I don't want to talk about *The Procrastinator,*" said Mr. Brougham. "You are much too tired."

"I beg your pardon? *I* am much too tired?"

"Yes, haven't you noticed? You look dreadful."

Lady Molly, whose gown was of practical brown wool, with a high neck and long sleeves, knew she did not look her best and she took Mr. Brougham's criticism in good humour.

"Thank you," she laughed. "But you are right—I'm very tired. I hadn't known what work it is to put on amateur theatricals."

"Do you regret the project?"

"Not entirely. No, I truly don't regret it at all. Such a difference as it makes in the castle!"

"How?" asked Mr. Brougham, intent on her explanation.

"Everyone bustling about. A schedule to maintain. Actual things to do, instead of endlessly talking to one's fellow residents. None of those tedious games of cards. All in all, I can happily recommend amateur theatricals to any hostess—they quite change the spirit of the winter and make entertaining far, far easier."

"You don't have to think up schemes for our amusement, for example?"

"If the play isn't a scheme for amusement, I don't know what it is!"

"Day-to-day schemes, I mean. Like nutting parties or expeditions to local sites of interest."

"Are you by any chance suggesting that I plan such a party?" asked Lady Molly.

"No. I think I should plan it. Or your sister. Or the butler—anyone but you."

Lady Molly chuckled. "I am too tired, but you do want a day in the open!"

Mr. Brougham sighed. He explained, as one might to a small child, "*I* don't want a day in the open. I can go shooting with your father whenever I like. But I think you should have a day in the open."

Lady Molly was touched by this concern for her health; she had indeed been unusually tired and irritable lately.

"But the rehearsing," she said, without conviction. "I

can't stop for a day just as people are learning their lines."

"*Some* people are learning their lines, you mean."

Lady Molly laughed again. Mr. Brougham rejoiced that he had made her laugh three times in five minutes.

"But do you seriously think we could take a day's holiday?"

Even as she spoke, Lady Molly wondered why she valued Mr. Brougham's advice so highly. She had conceived of this play as *her* project, and yet she could hardly bear those rehearsals at which he was not present. They were rare; Mr. Brougham took his responsibilities as prompter seriously. And he was almost always beside her at the end of the evening, to walk with her to the drawing room and talk over the progress of the day. He had not repeated his declaration of love, nor had he by word or gesture hinted at it. Lady Molly wondered why, but his silence would have troubled her more had she not been so busy. As it was, she was content to have him there, to laugh with her at an egregious error, to advise her about where the actors should stand in a complicated scene, to cajole the actors into a good humour after she had chastised them, and to comfort her when everything seemed to be going wrong. The play left her little time to talk to anyone, and she was glad of that. With Mr. Brougham beside her, reading the script or discussing the players, Lady Molly had little chance to speak to Sir Marius. Occasionally he had seemed disgruntled, but Lady Molly was hardly aware of that. She had deliberately narrowed her world; she would not think of her future; she allowed herself to think of nothing but the play as it should be performed on Christmas Eve.

"Yes, Lady Molly, I insist that you take a day off from rehearsing! Tell them all to memorise their lines in that day. You've been working them to the bone."

"I've been working them hard? Yes, I suppose I have. What shall it be, then? A nutting party?"

"Such deference! Do you like nutting parties?"

"One never finds enough nuts to make them worth the trouble. But the woods can be lovely this time of year."

"Well, then . . ." said Mr. Brougham, who sensed that it was time for them to return to the others.

"But what I would like most is not a nutting party, but a skating party," concluded Lady Molly. "Much more dashing and improper! But I daresay Aunt Amelia can be made to consent."

"If the water's properly frozen."

"It should be by now—but I'll ask Newcome." Lady Molly rose and, with one of her odd lapses into formality, thanked Mr. Brougham for his clever suggestion. She stopped and looked at him before walking away.

"But you haven't told me your opinion of amateur theatricals," she said. "Surely you've enjoyed this rehearsing?"

"I've enjoyed working on the play, yes, but I find it a peculiar pastime for a young lady."

Lady Molly sighed. "I do not, as you know, subscribe to your uncle's belief that amateur theatricals—or theatricals of any sort—are morally opprobrious. I conceive play-acting to be far more innocent an activity than the reckless gaming that is so often practised without condemnation. Play-acting is an admirable exercise in accommodation—working with so many people, one gains a sense of mutual endeavour and, to put it bluntly, some social poise that might otherwise elude one. What is more, true comedy—which is what is under question when we speak of amateur theatricals—is always uplifting. Morally dubious as many of the plays of King Charles's day are, they do arouse our sympathy for the good and demonstrate most vividly how even he who is at heart a good man may sin. And the comedies of the present day, those of Mr. Blaine, Mr. Fremantle, Mr. Sheridan, and a dozen less-talented others, are of course far more correct. Yet, even, if they were not so proper, we could learn much from them."

"I beg your pardon?"

"Shakespeare is the most improper playwright I know, and even his warmest scenes serve to illuminate the ways of the human mind."

Mr. Brougham was genuinely interested in Lady Molly's opinion; he had not expected so well reasoned a defence of theatre from a duke's daughter, who, after all, need defend herself to no one.

"Have you seen Mr. Bowdler's celebrated new edition of the Bard?" he asked. "All passages which might offend the ears of young ladies have been summarily excised. He renders Shakespeare a polite, tinkling poet of the last century—'correctly cold and regularly low.' Addison's 'Cato' has more poetic power than Bowdler's 'Lear'!"

"Of all things the most odious is such a mutilation! I was uncommonly fortunate, in that my father—"

Here Lady Molly grinned and lowered her voice. They stood only a few yards away from the rest of the company.

"My father," she continued, "seldom remarked that I spent many hours in his library. And I was blessed with an understanding governess. To judge from my own experience, Mr. Brougham, I shouldn't think most young ladies can understand the warmer passages of Shakespeare. And young men, to judge from my brother Jamie's experience, are unlikely to bother with Shakespeare."

"Catullus is far warmer," Mr. Brougham said. "Once one reaches a certain proficiency in Latin."

"I was never permitted to read Catullus," Lady Molly admitted. "Thus far was my governess vigilant. And my Latin was never very good. But I haven't made my point yet; I'm sorry to be prosing on like this."

"No, I'm extraordinarily interested."

"Not shocked?"

"No, not shocked. Do go on, Lady Molly."

"All I really wished to say was that I would far rather entrust my moral welfare to the genius whose name is revered all over the globe than to this unknown, self-righteous Mr. Bowdler! And that I sincerely believe the theatre to be of enormous benefit to our minds and souls."

Lady Molly stopped suddenly and looked round the room. The Contessa di Innamorati had sat down on one of the Chippendale chairs Lady Molly had borrowed from the west wing to use in her play, and the swarm of admirers that always accompanied her were crowding round her chair, waiting for her next deliciously accented witticism. Lord St. Omar was telling an apocryphal anecdote about his Grand Tour to Mrs. Townley and the two Fancot girls, Mrs. Townley and the elder Miss Fancot disbelieving, but young Sally Fancot hanging on his every word like Desdemona at the feet of her Moor. Tony Laverham hovered about this group, unable to gain a word or a glance from pretty Sally. Sir Marius and Lady Rich stood a few paces apart from the rest, at the very back of the stage; Sir Marius was laughing at something Lady Rich had said to him.

"I don't share your confidence, my dear," Mr. Brougham said, so softly that Lady Molly could barely hear him. "Do you truly believe that after acting in this play, or after seeing a thousand great tragedies, anybody's moral character will magically improve?"

The next day, Lady Molly sent out a footman to test the ice on the small lake in the home wood. He reported that the lake was safely frozen over, and Lady Molly told her father that she would like to have a skating party. The resources even at Seekings Castle were taxed by such a request, but servants were sent round to borrow skating blades from the neighbouring gentry.

The younger people at Seekings were all delighted with the plan, and Phoebe Townley even stopped by Lady Molly's bedchamber one evening before dinner to congratulate her on the idea.

"We all need a change," she told Lady Molly. "I'm so tired of rehearsing that I can barely pay attention to what I'm doing on stage. And poor Tony Laverham is exhausted with the effort of learning his lines."

"Yes, isn't it amazing. He tries and tries, and still can't learn them."

Lady Molly had not completed her _toilette_. Mrs. Townley sat on the low sofa before the fire and watched her friend submit to her abigail's ministrations. Lady Molly stood still as her maid fastened a string of pearls round her neck—"for we are dining quite *en famille* tonight, Phoebe, so I shan't bother with jewels," she called over her shoulder—and pinned up her curls.

"Sir Marius is improving, though," Mrs. Townley said. "He's almost word-perfect."

"Mr. Brougham should take credit for that," said Lady Molly. "Such a brow-beating as he gives Sir Marius!"

"Yes, Mr. Brougham never raises his voice—but he does somehow keep order. He cajoles everyone out of their bad tempers; the gentleman is everything that's agreeable."

Lady Molly's tone was light, but she immediately changed the subject.

"Phoebe, you haven't told me what you think of the production. Will it go off successfully, do you think?"

"Indubitably," said Mrs. Townley. "The play's a jewel, and the cast is quite remarkable. Even Sir Marius!"

"Why do you say *even* Sir Marius?" asked Lady Molly, her voice suddenly sharp.

"Simply because of his difficulty in memorising, Molly. But he's wonderfully amusing."

"On stage, perhaps."

"Why, Molly! Are you quarrelling with him?"

Lady Molly regretted her petulant exclamation. "No, of course not."

"You were so in love with him the year of our *début*," said Mrs. Townley. "I'll never forget the way you chattered, bubbling with happiness. Do you remember?"

"That was a long time ago. I remember, of course. But we were both very young."

"Your wedding will be in June?"

"Yes. That is, I think so. I'm not sure."

"Odd you should postpone it—after such a long betrothal."

"Phoebe, do stop prying! I don't see that my marriage is any concern of yours! And I don't wish to talk about it!"

Mrs. Townley rose and walked over to where Lady Molly still stood before the dressing table. The abigail had retreated to the far side of the room. Mrs. Townley slipped her arm through Lady Molly's.

"I'm sorry, Molly. You're right—it's no affair of mine. But I can't help being curious. It must be so hard for you, to see Sir Marius after so long a separation. And your feelings towards him would seem to have altered!"

"Altered? Altered how?" asked Lady Molly, pulling her arm out of Mrs. Townley's embrace.

"Molly, surely you know how differently you treat Sir Marius now," stammered Mrs. Townley. "The look in your eyes, your tone of voice, even. Everything's changed."

"I hardly think that you, who has proved such an abominable judge of character, should question my manner towards my *fiancé*. Your feelings for Mr. Townley have certainly changed, haven't they, Phoebe? Or is it merely his feelings for you?"

At this reference to Mr. Townley's notorious liaison with Lady Cowper, Mrs. Townley crimsoned. "I shall leave you now, Molly," she said. "I think, upon reflection, you will realise that I spoke as your friend."

Lady Molly was instantly contrite. "I know that, my dear. I'm sorry, Phoebe; I don't know why I spoke as I did. Forgive me, do! I just don't want to speak about Sir Marius."

"Very well," said Mrs. Townley, mollified. "Though that was an odious thing to say! Is that satin from Paris?"

Lady Molly admitted that her gown of cream-coloured satin was indeed from Paris—"Purchased two years ago, but don't tell anyone it's old!"—and the two friends went down to the drawing-room.

* * *

None of the older members of the party wanted to join Lady Molly's skating excursion. But when both the Contessa di Innamorati and Lady Rich declared their delight with the scheme, none of the younger people wanted to be left out. Newcome was able to obtain a sufficient number of blades to be strapped onto the skaters' shoes, and, shortly after luncheon, two days after Mr. Brougham had suggested it to Lady Molly, the expedition set forth.

The lake was at the far end of the home wood, but it was another crystalline day; despite the cold, no one minded the walk. Behind a protective screen of bushes, the ladies sat down on the rough benches Newcome had sent out to the wood and, with much giggling, strapped the double runners onto their shoes. The worst part of the expedition, Miss Fancot shrilly declared, was descending from the bench to the edge of the lake: "One can't keep from wobbling, and the gentlemen are watching!"

"Why don't you ask the gentlemen to help?" Lady Molly said tartly as she struggled with a loose strap.

Miss Fancot protested that she wouldn't dream of such an imposition upon the gentlemen's good humour, but her younger sister gratefully accepted Tony Laverham's arm, and Miss Fancot, left alone to teeter down the slope, regretted her statement.

All the other ladies permitted the gentlemen to assist them. Lord St. Omar escorted Mrs. Townley, Lord Silverton won the Contessa's arm, Sir Marius helped Lady Rich down the slope, and Mr. Brougham, of course, waited by Lady Molly's side as she fought with her strap.

"Shall I do it?" he asked.

"Mr. Brougham!"

As he had genuinely forgotten the impropriety of such a suggestion, Mr. Brougham was apologetic.

"I do beg your pardon. I merely meant—well, I wasn't thinking, and you seemed to be having trouble."

"That's all right," said Lady Molly, recovering from

her first shock. "I am having trouble. And, do you know, perhaps you would be able to fasten it."

Mr. Brougham glanced round the wood. "No one can see," he assured her.

"Very well, then," said Lady Molly. She extended her foot in its dainty Spanish leather half-boot. Mr. Brougham knelt before her and began to unknot the strap. Lady Molly smiled at his air of fierce concentration. As he rewound the strap about her foot, he suddenly laughed.

"What is it?" asked Lady Molly.

"I was just thinking," he said, without looking up, "that this might be the right occasion for putting a question to you."

"Oh, you were?"

"It's the right position, anyway. Ah, there you are," he said as he buckled the strap into place. "That should hold." He looked up and met her eyes. He took the hand she held out towards him, but spoke without rising.

"Molly, my dear, my very dear, you know what I want to say." After this opening, Mr. Brougham stopped, unable to continue.

Lady Molly gently prompted him. "I think I do," she said. "But I wish you would say it. You must be very cold, kneeling in the snow like that."

Mr. Brougham, who was indeed very cold, stood up and then pulled Lady Molly to stand facing him.

"Molly, you know I want you to marry me! And you know damn well why I can't ask you to! What do you want me to say?"

Lady Molly could not meet his eyes. "I suppose I want you to say that you love me."

Mr. Broughman tightened his grasp on her shoulders. "That's not right, Molly. You shouldn't want to hear those words from anyone but your dashing Sir Marius. Why should I say that to you?"

He dared not raise his voice, because of the people on the lake a few yards away, but he shook her violently.

Lady Molly, precariously balancing on her skates, fell against him. Mr. Brougham pulled her into his arms and kissed her. After a few minutes, he lifted his head.

"Now will you tell that fool you won't marry him?" He tried to push her away from him. "Go tell him!"

Shaken as she was, Lady Molly had to laugh. "Kit, would you please calm down? In another moment you'll have knocked me into a snowdrift. And I can't possibly walk to the lake by myself."

She still had her arms round his neck and Mr. Brougham could not disentwine himself. He kissed her again.

"If I escort you to the lake, will you break your engagement?" he asked in a more reasonable tone.

"If you don't escort me to the lake, I shall scream for help," Lady Molly told him. "And whether you do so or not, I shall tell Sir Marius at the nearest opportunity that I will not marry him."

"You wouldn't like to do it now? Just casually call it out to him? Then we needn't go down to the lake at all."

"We must go down," said Lady Molly. "Now," she added firmly, as Mr. Brougham tried to kiss her again.

"If Sir Marius happened to look this way and see us *in flagrante delicto,* wouldn't your engagement be at an end? Without the need for any tedious explanations."

"I should think the explanations, in that case, would be even more difficult," Lady Molly replied drily. Then she turned in his arms. "But they can't truly see us? You don't think they can?"

"You are going to fall into a snowbank. Do try to have a little faith in me, Molly. Much as I would like to, I am not going to kiss you when anyone else is looking— at least not until I get a chance to ask you to marry me."

"You have a chance. Ask me!" Lady Molly said without shame.

"You deserve better than a conditional declaration."

"Conditional?"

"If you don't marry Sir Marius Wadman . . ."

"Oh, I see. We must go, then. The others will be missing us."

After one more kiss, Mr. Brougham gave Lady Molly his arm and helped her round the wall of bushes and down the short slope to the lake.

Chapter Ten

"Now you go talk to Sir Marius while I put my skates on," said Mr. Brougham, launching Lady Molly onto the lake.

He expected her to stumble and clutch at the nearest person, as the other ladies had done, but Lady Molly glided away, her hands confidently tucked in her sable muff.

So happy was she that the exhaustion of the last few weeks fell away from her. Her cheeks glowed with exercise; her frock of blue cashmere became her; and the sables wrapped round it were the envy of every other lady. Lady Rich had, like Lady Molly, been given furs on her twenty-first birthday by the Duke, but hers were necessarily several years older and shabbier. Lady Molly could have sung as she skated round the lake; all the doubts that had afflicted her for weeks floated away. She remembered the daze in which she had moved after Sir Marius's first kiss so many years before, and came close to shuddering. That was champagne, and flattery, she thought to herself. This is love.

Obedient to instructions, she skated quickly until she caught up with Sir Marius, who had Miss Fancot on one arm and Lady Rich on the other. She watched his handsome face incline to hear Lady Rich's latest *bon mot* and suddenly felt sick. But she skated up and greeted them gaily.

"Juliana, you've lost none of your prowess! This was always our favourite sport," Lady Molly explained to Sir Marius.

"Did the lake freeze over every winter?" Miss Fancot asked.

"It seems that way, when I look back. Though I'm sure it didn't."

"Molly was always the best of us," Lady Rich assured Sir Marius. "Far better than Jamie, even."

Lady Molly began to feel silly. She couldn't even take Sir Marius's arm, as he was burdened with two ladies already, and she saw no way in which she could speak to him alone. At that moment, Mr. Brougham skated up. Just as he arrived, Miss Fancot stumbled.

"Allow me," he said, taking her arm. "And Lady Rich, if I may?"

Lady Rich gave him a quizzical look, then glanced back at Sir Marius. "As you see, Sir Marius, I must desert you."

"Yes, let's leave Sir Marius and his beloved alone for a few minutes," cooed Miss Fancot. "So little as they must see of one another."

Miss Fancot, who was sincerely fond of Lady Molly, could not understand why all four of her auditors jumped at her remark. She racked her brain, trying to decide where her error lay. Mr. Brougham's smooth interposition, after his first shock, reassured her that the consternation writ on his face, and Lady Molly's, must have been illusory.

"Yes, let's do just that," he said as he deftly steered his two ladies away. "And I can entertain you with the grisly tale of how I fell through the ice while skating in Northumberland."

Miss Fancot squealed as the three of them skated away. "Oh no, did you really? What a horrid thought!"

Lady Molly gingerly took Sir Marius's arm. She looked across the lake to where the Contessa, resplendent in a red pelisse with ermine trim, moved slowly and majestically over the ice, with what looked like a royal entourage of attendant gentlemen skating beside her. Then Lady Molly gazed to the left, at Mr. Brougham and his two ladies, before speaking to Sir Marius.

"Sir Marius, I am glad to have this chance to speak to you without auditors."

"Dashed rude of Miss Fancot to point that out," Sir Marius interrupted. "The girl's got no sense of how to behave in society. She's a homely thing, too."

Lady Molly had always regarded Miss Fancot with indifference. She was difficult to converse with and awkward at dances, but all in all Lady Molly thought her an inoffensive young lady. This revelation of Sir Marius's temper shocked her and made it easier for her to say what she wished.

"We have been very little together," she began.

"That's not true, Molly, my dear. Not alone together, but I've seen you every day during the rehearsals."

"Yes, but . . ."

"Look, Molly, I'm sorry if you feel I've been neglecting you, but I've been dashed busy. Memorising my lines, for one thing."

"You can't have been working very hard at that," Lady Molly snapped back. Then, with horror, she realised that she had lost control of the conversation. Sir Marius was angry with her before she had even broached the subject of their betrothal.

"You've gotten so you can't think of anything but your

play! Too much telling people what to do, that's what's wrong with you," he snapped at her.

Lady Molly felt guilty. She began to murmur an apology, then she remembered Mr. Brougham's kiss. Invigorated, she abandoned all solicitude for Sir Marius's sensibilities.

"I'm sure there's more than that wrong with me. And I really don't care. I've come to the conclusion, Sir Marius, that we've been wrong for five years."

Sir Marius, who had forgotten the exact number of years he had been acquainted with Lady Molly, looked blank.

Lady Molly knew she had to speak more plainly. She looked down at her feet, trying to avoid his eye as she spoke the words that would sever them forever, and she promptly tripped.

Sir Marius helped her regain her balance, then said, "There, now, Molly, would you please be more careful? You can't do everything, my dear."

Lady Molly did not like his proprietary arm round her waist, and she finally spoke plainly.

"I am not your dear! I mean, I don't want to be. I should never have said I was! Let go of me!"

She pulled away from him, nearly tripping again as she did so.

"I don't want to marry you. I shan't marry you. And I don't think you want to marry me, so don't tell me I'm behaving badly," Lady Molly said, not knowing where the words came from.

Blood rushed to Sir Marius's cheeks. "I say, Molly," he protested. "I never thought you'd take it like this."

"Like what?" demanded Lady Molly, some six feet away from him. "I am perfectly calm, and I am asking you to release me from our engagement."

"It's not as though I'd done anything so terrible. Would you please stop and think about what you are doing? I don't like you to make a decision in a fit of temper."

"I am not having a fit of temper!"

Sir Marius caught up with her and made the mistake of reaching out to grasp her arm. With a backhanded sweep of her arm, she pushed him away, throwing her sable muff halfway across the lake as she did so.

Mr. Brougham, having deposited Miss Fancot by the shore where she could watch everyone else skating, and having relinquished Lady Rich to Lord Dewhurst's chaperonage, had been watching Lady Molly. When she repulsed Sir Marius and her muff sailed away, he rushed forward, scooped up the muff, and sped to Lady Molly's side.

"Your muff, I think?"

Sir Marius glowered a few feet off, and Mr. Brougham's spirits rose at his obvious discomfiture. Pleased with the world and with himself, he attempted a bow as Lady Molly slipped her hands into the muff. The result was disastrous.

Sir Marius skated off as Lady Molly helped Mr. Brougham to his feet.

"Would you please stop laughing? Stand still and let me brush this snow off!" Lady Molly commanded.

"I can't help it! What a scene! Did you see the expression on his face? What did you say to him?"

"Thanks to your interruption," Lady Molly said, "I'm not sure but that I'm still engaged to him."

"He looked angry with you," said Brougham, sobering immediately.

"He was angry. I'm afraid I didn't handle the matter with delicacy."

"What did you say?"

"Oh, Kit, it's not your concern."

"It certainly is, my girl. Now let's skate along very quickly, before anyone else joins us. And tell me what you said."

"I told him I didn't want to marry him."

"Just like that?"

"Well, then he had the audacity to say that I was indulging in a fit of temper!"

"So then you did indulge in a fit of temper?"

"Yes, that's when I lost my muff and you entered the scene."

"Stumbling to the rescue, I should call it," said Mr. Brougham ruefully. "My buckskins will never be the same. It sounds like you made a mess of it. He didn't release you from the betrothal?"

"I've never done this before! How was I supposed to know he would ask me to reconsider?"

"He has to agree to dissolve the betrothal, you know. If a lady regrets her decision, the gentleman must accede."

"Of course he'll accede to my request. He's not going to force me to marry him. If you hadn't interrupted, maybe the betrothal would be dissolved by now."

"If I hadn't interrupted," said Mr. Brougham, "poor Sir Marius wouldn't have had the least idea why he was so summarily rejected."

"Oh, do you think he's guessed?"

Mr. Brougham, with his left hand, brushed a curl off his beloved's forehead. "I should think everyone's guessed, my dear."

"No, they can't have." Lady Molly looked round the lake and could see no one watching. "They all think we're having an *à suivi* flirtation."

"A what?" Mr. Brougham demanded.

"Isn't that the correct term? For a reckless affair?"

"For a reckless affair, my lovely innocent, yes. For what we are having, no. I have assured you many times that my intentions are strictly honourable. And if you cherish the least doubt of that, you oughtn't be skating alone with me when the light is quickly fading and, if we go up that brook a few yards, no one can see us."

"Kit, don't be absurd. I can't behave like a guttersnipe. All those people are going to want to go back soon."

"Guttersnipes don't embrace in the snow," Mr. Brougham said. "And I didn't suggest anything, anyway. I was demonstrating to you what dishonourable intentions might be like."

Lady Molly lifted a hand to his cheek, "Not exactly demonstrating," she said softly, "Another time. Now, Kit, what am I to do?"

Mr. Brougham kissed her hand. "Do about what?" he asked. "Which of your many problems?"

"Kit, how do I truly break this engagement?"

"You aren't going to break this engagement. You're going to marry me."

"I know that. But we aren't ever going to be engaged if I don't find some way to break off with Sir Marius. Do I have to talk to him alone? And how can I arrange that?"

Mr. Brougham frowned. "I don't want you to see him alone. I have an irrational mistrust of the man."

"What should I do, then? It seems cowardly to ask Father to talk to him—and I'm not at all sure Father would do it."

"Why not? Your father doesn't want you to marry that court-card, does he?"

"He gave his consent five years ago."

"I'm a much better match. Will you mind being Lady Mary Brougham and Mr. Brougham? When my uncle dies, I'll be Annesley, you know. You'll like the place. Miles from anywhere, but lovely. The Hall's much smaller than Seekings—no one but Devonshire or the Churchills can compete with this place—but it's much prettier. Just a hundred years old, but a perfect Palladian facade, and beautifully situated on a rise."

"I looked it all up in Carey's guide weeks ago," said Lady Molly.

Mr. Brougham smiled at her and pressed her arm more

closely. There was no excuse for Lady Molly and Mr. Brougham to linger together any longer and Lady Molly, afraid of comment, insisted that they part. She joined her brother and Mrs. Townley while Mr. Brougham entered the flock round the Contessa. They were both careful not to pass Sir Marius, who was speaking earnestly to Lady Rich.

The light was indeed fading by now, and soon several footmen arrived from the castle. Bearing torches, they led the party back to the castle, up the narrow path through the home wood.

Lady Molly walked beside her friend Phoebe Townley. They conversed idly for some time, remarking on the cold and the snow that had begun to fall. Then, as they emerged from the wood and Mrs. Townley saw Tony Laverham bearing down on them, she said softly, "There's no time to talk now. But I want to assure you that I will be here to listen to any problem."

"What makes you think I have any problem?" said Lady Molly, not ungratefully.

Mrs. Townley looked at her friend and smiled. "What worries me," she admitted, "is how happy you seem."

Lady Molly was tempted to confide in her friend, but Tony Laverham joined the two ladies just then. The conversation perforce became general, but Lady Molly did hiss in Mrs. Townley's ear, "Why does that worry you?"

Mrs. Townley smiled and shrugged. "Just because," she said and turned to speak to Mr. Laverham.

Chapter Eleven

"Where are the joy and mirth that made this town a joy on earth?" Miss Fancot warbled. "Gone, gone with thee, Robin Adair," she concluded, holding the final two notes for an intolerable minute.

The dozen people seated in the blue drawing room of Seekings Castle applauded weakly as Miss Fancot stepped down from the pianoforte.

"Will you sing, Molly?" Lady Amelia Drayton asked. "She has the most delightful voice, although her playing was never more than passable," she confided to Lady Wellburn.

"Yes, Lady Mary, you must sing," said Lady Wellburn, undaunted by this warning. Lady Wellburn turned to face Lady Amelia, who sat on her right. She tapped Lady Amelia's arm and declared, in a whisper that could be heard by everyone in the room, "She's a prime favourite with me, your niece."

Lady Molly smothered a smile and rose. "I should be

delighted to sing, Lady Wellburn. Aunt Amelia, will you play for me?"

"Allow me to do so, Lady Amelia," Mr. Brougham said quickly, before Lady Amelia could disarrange the net of shawls in which she reposed.

Lady Wellburn raised her lorgnette. "And is your playing more than passable, young man?"

"I hope so." Mr. Brougham moved to the pianoforte. "What would you like, Lady Wellburn?"

"Yes, have you any preference?" asked Lady Molly.

Lady Wellburn beamed through her lorgnette at the two young people. "I shouldn't venture to tell you what to play," she cooed, obviously pleased to be consulted. "But I can't abide Scottish airs."

Miss Fancot, whose rendition of Lady Carolina Nairne's wistful ballad had exacerbated the musical sensibilities of everyone in the room, blushed. Lady Molly, who wanted everyone to be happy that evening, looked reproachfully at Lady Wellburn.

"Burns is frequently quite indecent," said Lady Molly, "and much of the dialect is incomprehensible, but there are some Scottish songs that touch one's heart as no English melody can."

"There are a few of unassailable purity," Lady Wellburn admitted. "And Carolina Nairne's verses are among the prettiest I know."

Miss Fancot (like her sister Sally, who persisted in following Lord St. Omar about the castle) was not gifted with much perception and took these tributes at their face value. The hot tears that had stood in her eyes disappeared. "'Lochaber No More' is even more charming," she said eagerly.

"Would you like to sing it for us, Miss Fancot?" Mr. Brougham asked.

Even Miss Fancot could not mistake the rustle of dismay that ran round the room, although she was spared the Contessa's cruel exclamation in Italian. Mr. Brougham, who knew enough Italian to distinguish what the Contessa had said, choked slightly.

"No, I think Lady Molly should take a turn," said Miss Fancot. "I am so longing to hear her." Rewarded with a sparkling smile from Mr. Brougham, Miss Fancot retired to a seat in a dark corner, next to her mother. Lady Molly and Mr. Brougham began to examine the pile of music on the pianoforte.

"No Burns," he reminded her in an undertone.

"And no Italian," said Lady Molly. "I don't trust my accent, and the Contessa's in the room."

"What about a Templeton Blaine song?" asked Mr. Brougham.

"I don't think we have the music to any of them," said Lady Molly.

"I usually play from memory," said Mr. Brougham. "I think I could manage it."

To his chagrin, Lady Molly said she thought they'd all had enough of Templeton Blaine. Rooting through the pile, she pulled out a sheet and placed it triumphantly on the music rack.

"Do you know this?" she asked, her eyes dancing. "I've always been fond of it."

"Suckling, isn't it? I know the melody. Shall we?"

Mr. Brougham began to play the lilting melody. He played well, with a light, sure touch and pronounced rhythm. After a moment, Lady Molly's rich contralto joined in.

> *"I prithee send me back my heart,*
> *Since I cannot have thine;*
> *For if from yours you will not part,*
> *Why then shouldst thou have mine?"*

Several people had sung earlier that evening, and everyone in the room was tired. The Duke, just before Lady Molly had started singing, could have been heard muttering that it was past time to go to bed. But Lady Molly had by far the best voice of any of the ladies, Mr. Brougham's playing complemented it perfectly, and neither of them had ever performed as well before. The long drawing room was hushed as Lady Molly repeated the gay love song that had been written almost two hundred years before.

> "Yet now I think on't, let it lie,
> To find it were in vain;
> For th' hast a thief in either eye
> Would steal it back again
>
> Why should two hearts in one breast lie,
> And yet not lodge together?
> O love, where is thy sympathy,
> If thus our breasts thou sever?"

Sir Marius Wadman had been very much occupied with his own affairs since arriving at Seekings; this evening was the first time he noted the intimacy between Lady Molly and Mr. Brougham. He had recognised the determination in Lady Molly's voice when she had accosted him during the skating party. He had asked her to reconsider withdrawing from their betrothal, as an immediate reaction to a surprising request from her, but he was not displeased with her decision. As a gentleman, he could do nothing to terminate an understanding with a young lady, but his Jamaican inheritance had proved larger than he had expected. Lady Molly's money would make less of a difference in his life, and she was no longer the adoring, endearing girl he had left behind him, but was a self-possessed young lady with an irksome air of superiority. Sir Marius knew their betrothal was now only a formality on verge of dissolution, and looking at Lady Molly as she sang, he realised why the dissolution was necessary. Being a genuinely good-humoured man, he did not resent the glow Mr. Brougham's presence brought to Lady Molly. He was glad they both looked so happy; in that moment, Sir Marius dismissed Lady Molly from his mind for once and for all.

> *"But love is such a mystery,*
> *I cannot find it out;*
> *For when I think I'm best resolv'd,*
> *I then am most in doubt."*

Mr. Brougham knew better than to spoil the enchantment by joining his voice to Lady Molly's, but he murmured the words under his breath as she sang the final verse.

> *"Then farewell care, and farewell woe,*
> *I will no longer pine;*
> *For I'll believe I have her heart*
> *As much as she has mine."*

This time the final note of the song was not prolonged. A few chords and it was over, Lady Molly smilingly refusing all pleas for an encore. "We're all tired," she said. "And I think my father would like to retire."

The Duke was lost in a reverie.

"You're going to tell her her mother could sing like that, eh, Duke?" said Lady Wellburn. "You look lost in the past. I do that often myself."

The Duke recalled himself with an effort. He gave Lady Wellburn a faint, sweet smile. "Yes, I was thinking of the past," he said with weary courtesy. "It was not, however, the Duchess who could sing."

After the musical entertainment, Lady Molly was recruited to make a fourth at whist. Mr. Brougham, realising that he would get no further chance to speak to her alone that evening, left the rest of the party and found his way to the library, where he hoped he could smoke a *cigarillo* without offending any ladies. The library door was ajar, and Mr. Brougham had no hesitation about walking in. His feet made no noise on the Gobelin carpet, and it was not until he coughed that Sir Marius and Lady Rich jumped apart.

Mr. Brougham displayed more embarrassment than the couple he had surprised in a clandestine embrace. Sir Marius started laughing when he saw Mr. Brougham, and Lady Rich merely smiled.

"Good evening," she said. She noticed the *cigarillo* he had already extracted from his case. "You came in here to smoke?"

"Yes," said Mr. Brougham. "I can't think Lady Amelia would permit me to do so in the drawing room or the card room."

"You're quite right. The library is a far better place to indulge in secret vices."

Mr. Brougham had to laugh at Lady Rich's gleeful expression. She was absurdly pleased with herself, twisting her finger in one blond curl and looking up at Mr. Brougham through half-closed eyes.

"Then I shall leave you to yours," he said. "Good evening, Sir Marius. Your servant, Lady Rich."

_____*Chapter Twelve*

Later that evening, as Mr. Brougham was reading the *Guide to the Turf* before retiring to bed, there was a rap on his chamber door. He opened the door to Sir Marius, widening his eyes as he took in the full glory of his guest's frogged and brocaded smoking jacket.

Sir Marius mumbled a request to enter and speak with him. Mr. Brougham had never been able to dislike Sir Marius, much as he resented his presence and conduct. Taking pity on the tongue-tied older man, Mr. Brougham ushered him in with a smile.

"I expected you'd come by," said Mr. Brougham. "I had Newcome send up some cognac."

Sir Marius took a glass and sipped at it several times before speaking. In the firelight, he looked younger than Mr. Brougham had even seen him. His hair looked ever golden against the high collar of his dark purple smoking jacket, and his face was still boyish. And when he finally looked up and grinned, Mr. Brougham could understand why both Lady Molly and Lady Rich had found him charming.

"I suppose I don't need to tell you what I've come about," said Sir Marius.

"No, you don't. I assume you want to offer some sort of explanation for your behaviour. Although it is the Duke—and Lord Rich—to whom you owe an explanation."

Sir Marius stiffened. "You needn't take it that way, Brougham."

"You can't have expected that I would regard your conduct as anything less than execrable!"

Sir Marius bridled at this bluntness, and took a large gulp of his brandy. Then, almost visibly, an idea came to him. His aspect brightened and he leaned forward to address Mr. Brougham.

"But your conduct hasn't been too honourable, either, has it, Brougham? I'd wager you've kissed my intended wife."

Sir Marius's tone was not offensive: he was amused at the thought. Mr. Brougham found this indifference annoying.

"You shouldn't be smiling like that," he said, rising from his chair. He walked to the far side of the room and stared, unseeing, at a pretty water-colour landscape executed by a great-aunt of Lady Molly. Sir Marius, still smiling at his own clever riposte, was startled when Mr. Brougham whirled round and abruptly addressed him.

"You ought to be angry," said Mr. Brougham, drawling slightly. The calm in his voice was at variance with his angry stance. He had expected this visit, but he had not yet decided what he would say to Sir Marius—whether he would take it on himself to inform Sir Marius of Lady Molly's altered sentiments, whether he would promise to reveal to no one the incident he had witnessed, and what, indeed, was his opinion of Sir Marius and Lady Rich's *affaire.* He maintained control over his voice with difficulty as he said, "Dammit, you're the one she's supposed to be marrying."

"She's a fine girl, Brougham," said Sir Marius. "I'm very fond of Lady Molly."

Mr. Brougham could stand no more. "Oh, God! I might as well tell you that she has not the least intention of going through with this betrothal."

"Is that so? Can't say it comes as a surprise. You two have been smelling of April and May. Not that I mind, you understand, but you can't blame me for what I've been doing."

Mr. Brougham knew that this was not an official termination of the betrothal, but his heart nevertheless leapt with relief at having finally confronted Sir Marius. He refilled Sir Marius's glass.

"Molly may be betrothed to you, but Juliana is married to Lord Rich," he patiently explained. "And my intentions are quite honourable. But your behaviour, after all, isn't my concern. All that worries me is the humiliation for Lady Molly should your name become publicly linked with Lady Rich's."

"What, after she's jilted me for you! I can't grant you that would be too humiliating."

"No, in a few months, I suppose not. But she won't like it if people know you were carrying on before the engagement was abandoned."

Sir Marius waved his hand in a dismissive gesture. "No one will know that, my dear chap. Why aren't you having more of this brandy? Excellent cellar Chettam has."

"People will know soon enough if you continue to retire to the library after dinner," Mr. Brougham said.

Sir Marius admitted the justice of this observation. He grumbled for some minutes about the difficulty—which Mr. Brougham knew all too well—of having an uninterrupted, private conversation during the Christmas season at Seekings. Mr. Brougham said soothingly that matters would be easier once he and Lady Rich were back in London.

Sir Marius was not consoled. "But Rich is returning from Canada in a month or so," he said. "I can't tell you how Juliana is dreading that! The old man doesn't care for her at all. Never forgiven her for not giving him an heir."

"How Gothic," Mr. Brougham murmured. He was impressed, however, by the degree of affection Sir Marius seemed to have for Lady Rich. Sir Marius poured himself a third brandy and waxed eloquent on Lord Rich's lack of appreciation for his clever and accomplished wife. In Sir Marius's estimation, it seemed, the whole of London failed to appreciate Lady Rich at her true worth. "She's brainy, don't you see. That's why they gossip about her. She's no worse than half the peeresses of Britain. But she's so devilish clever. That's what they can't forgive her. That's why she's called fast."

Sir Marius's wholehearted admiration of Lady Rich was quite endearing, Mr. Brougham thought. Abominable as their disregard for Lady Molly was, the two were not at all a bad couple. Reflecting on this, Mr. Brougham devised a scheme. He poured Sir Marius a fourth brandy and himself a second.

"I don't say she'll have you, mind, but if the lady's agreeable, Sir Marius, why don't you elope?" asked Mr. Brougham.

As the abigail brushed Lady Molly's hair (one hundred strokes before bedtime), a note was slipped under her bedroom door. Lady Molly saw its arrival in her mirror. She sent her maid to fetch a bottle of scent from the adjoining dressing-room, snatched up the letter, and threw it behind the row of books that stood on the table by the door. When she had dabbed on a few drops of the unwanted scent, she persuaded her maid to go to bed, promising that she herself would be in bed within the half-hour. As soon as the door closed behind the abigail, Lady Molly seized the letter and tore it open. She walked over to the window and there, by the light of the six-pronged candelabrum, read Sir Marius's brief note absolving her of any responsibility towards him.

"I have been informed that your sentiments about our union may have altered," he had written, only to lapse quickly from this formal tone. "I should have guessed this would happen when I first saw you with Kit Brougham. Nice fellow, that. I'm sure you'll be happy. Juliana brought him down here, so I'm sure she'll be happy with your news. I'll send announcement of severance to papers tomorrow, unless you say otherwise. Yours, etc., Marius Wadman."

Lady Molly chuckled over the prose style. Sir Marius's letters leaned one way and then the other, and the lines staggered diagonally across the page. His handwriting was round, unformed, with an attempt at ornateness in the dashingly crossed *t*'s and the oversized capital letters. Her relief at escaping marriage to a grown man who could produce such a composition outweighed her indignation with Mr. Brougham for taking matters into his own hands, which was clearly what had happened.

It was not until she picked up the letter for a second perusal, lying in bed and about to snuff out her last candle, that she began to worry. Why had Sir Marius used Lady Rich's Christian name? And why had he mentioned her at all? Lady Molly reminded herself that, as her own experience years before testified, Sir Marius was given to sudden intimacy. Then she realised what that might mean. She reread the letter, for the third time, with a new suspicion. By the time she finished her examination of Sir Marius's few lines, she knew without any doubt or hesitation.

Dissatisfied as she was with Sir Marius, it can never be pleasant to learn that one's sister has stolen one's *fiancé;* Lady Molly's first emotion was wrath. A hundred conversations and scenes came into her mind: Sir Marius and Juliana playing piquet after supper, skating together on the little lake, and kissing each other during rehearsal as the exigencies of their *rôles* demanded. The image she saw most clearly, though, was that instant that Mr. Brougham had noted, when the light streamed down on all three of them and Sir Marius and Lady Rich had stood side by side to face her complaint.

"Kit told me all along not to marry him," Lady Molly said aloud in her empty room. Had he known of this liaison? she wondered. But Sir Marius had not yet returned from Jamaica when Mr. Brougham had first told her not to marry him. Then Lady Molly thought of the particularly repellant possibility that Sir Marius and Lady Rich had had some sort of understanding even before he had left for Jamaica, while he was courting Lady Molly, and that all London had known of it.

It took Lady Molly less than ten minutes to decide that she would not be able to sleep that night until she told her sister what she thought of her. That she no longer wished to marry Sir Marius was irrelevant to her fury. Juliana had had no way of knowing the state of Lady Molly's feelings for Sir Marius; Juliana had behaved very badly.

Lady Molly pulled on her dressing gown, knotted its cord about her waist, slipped on her fur-lined pantofles, and set off on the long journey to Juliana's bedchamber.

There was no logic behind the assignment of rooms in Seekings Castle, as could be testified by any visitor who had attempted to find his way unescorted from one room to another. Lady Rich, when a child, had requested a room in the north tower that was distinguished with Chinese wallpaper, and so Lady Molly had to traverse three galleries, the grand staircase, two lesser flights of stairs, and the earl's arcade before she reached her destination. All this chilly perambulation gave Lady Molly ample time to ponder the cause of her fury.

Oddly, the element that gave her most pause in her assessment of Lady Rich's conduct was one she had not even thought of in her first interpretation of the circumstances of this imbroglio. She had completely forgotten about Lord Rich. Much of London did so habitually, but it could not be denied that he had a certain significance in the arrangement of affairs at Seekings. Not that Lady Rich considered him for more than a few breaths before she did whatever she wanted. But Lady Molly reflected long over Lord Rich.

She had never, as a girl, understood why her lovely sister, so toasted and besought, had singled out Lord Rich from her crowd of admirers. He was an earl, and there were few dukes available that season. The deaf Duke of Devonshire seemed uninterested in marriage to anyone. Of the royal dukes, Clarence had come close to offering for Juliana Drayton—he admired blondes, and the Drayton fortune would have plumped his ever-empty pockets— but he had sheered off at the last minute, frightened by her volatility, it was said. While Juliana might have liked to be married to the third in line for the throne, the Duke of Chettam, who disapproved of the entire dynasty, was immensely relieved when the alliance fell through. Lord Rich might seem even less prepossessing than the corpulent Prince, the Duke had explained to Lady Molly, but his family tree was less tainted with instability and vulgarity.

Lord Rich's lineage was impeccable; his family was not of equal eminence with the Draytons, but then no more than a handful in the kingdom were. His income was highly satisfactory, and his character was self-effacing. That he resembled a cod and had about as much conversation, in Lady Molly's adolescent denunciation, could not weigh against such sterling qualifications for a husband, the Duke said, only half jesting. Juliana, a giddy girl at the time, seemed to have made her choice on rank alone, but the Duke suspected that might prove a blessing. Lord Rich could be relied on to behave like a gentleman at all times. On the basis of two reprehensible incidents—one with a young curate in the parish of King's Drayton when Juliana was not yet sixteen, and one with the drawing master at the boarding school to which he had bundled her off—the Duke felt that such forbearance on the part of her future husband would be necessary. Lord Rich's appointment to a diplomatic mission to Canada on behalf of His Majesty's government was the fortunate circumstance with which the Duke credited the marriage's duration for six years (no one had had the temerity to suggest that Lady Rich, three years married, might care to accompany her husband to the Americas).

The Duke had regarded Lord Rich's complacency as fortunate; Lady Molly, contemplating it for the first time, found it disgusting. She had never before recognised that her sister might well be, by the accepted rules of society, an immoral woman. Lady Molly's pace flagged as she struggled with this idea. She had reached the earl's arcade and she had not the least idea what she could say to Juliana.

She remembered other times when she had made this journey: when her sister had commandeered the remnant of Norwich silk she had wanted for doll dresses; when her sister had convinced the Duke that Lady Molly's old hacking pony ought to be sent to pasture; when her sister had repeated to Fanny Cartwright, the neighbouring squire's giggly daughter, the news of their cousin Charlotte Hadley's betrothal, which Lady Molly had confidentially imparted to her.

Such confrontations had never succeeded. Juliana had always had the hopeless advantage of three years' superiority. Juliana had only to drawl out an apology for having so distressed her dear little sister, and Lady Molly would regret having come to see her. Even worse were the occasions on which Juliana refused to comprehend her sister's complaint, forcing Lady Molly to reiterate it repeatedly in terms that sounded increasingly petty. But the worst of all were the times when Juliana would not acknowledge that there was anything out of the ordinary in a midnight visit from her sister. Chattering smoothly, Juliana would be so gracious that Lady Molly did not dare broach the subject of her grievance and would find herself gently edged out into the corridor without having so much as glared at her odious sister.

Remembering these occasions, Lady Molly began to feel some trepidation. By the time she reached the hall off which her sister's room lay, she bitterly regretted the impulse that had driven her from her bedchamber. But she reminded herself of the uncomfortable walk she had made. Squaring her jaw, she strode almost up to Lady Rich's door before she heard the voices inside.

Leaping backwards as if she had stepped on glass or seem an adder, she ran down the corridor and away from her sister's room, blessing the heavy carpeting that muffled her departure.

Lady Molly had no doubt as to her sister's interlocutor. She cursed her own *naïveté*, furious that it had not once occurred to her in that long, cold walk that Juliana might not be alone. The repulsion she had felt at the abstract thought of her sister's misbehaviour was nothing to her misery now that she had been confronted with evidence of it. That Sir Marius should be permitted Juliana's bedchamber, the bedchamber she had had since childhood, could have only one interpretation. Lady Molly cried silently as she walked through the interminable halls and stairways back to her room.

The candle she was carrying blew out in the earl's arcade, but Lady Molly did not regret it. Her progress was impeded, but she was less likely to be accosted by an overzealous servant. No such servant was about, however. All the candelabra in the public rooms of the castle were extinguished. Lady Molly, tears dripping down her cheeks, moved blindly through the great rooms, like the ghost of her great-great-grandmother that was said to haunt Seekings.

It was a night to believe in ghosts. Moonlight flashed between clouds to illuminate her way and the great house creaked and murmured behind her. Lady Molly almost fancied herself a ghost.

She screamed aloud when Mr. Brougham lay a hand on her arm.

Chapter Thirteen

"It's only I," he said. "How fortunate that there are no bedchambers in this gallery! But why did you scream?"

Then, as the clouds lifted from the moon and a beam of light irradiated the gallery, Mr. Brougham saw her face. "Molly!" he exclaimed, and put his hands up to frame her face. She twisted away from his caress, then collapsed into his arms.

"Oh, Kit, I'm so glad to see you," she sobbed. "But what in heaven's name are you doing here?"

"Waiting for you."

"But how . . . ?"

"I thought I should warn you that I—well, Molly, I hope you won't be angry with me, but I told Sir Marius that I had reason to believe you regretted the betrothal."

Lady Molly dismissed this confession. "I know. He sent me a note. And I knew you must have spoken to him. But what are you doing here?"

Mr. Brougham had the grace to blush. "I thought you

ought to know as soon as possible. Rather, to be honest, I wanted you to know as soon as possible. So I went to your bedchamber."

"Kit, you didn't!"

"No one saw me. And I'd enquired as to where it was days ago."

There was a bitter note in Lady Molly's laugh. "So experienced as you are at these intrigues!"

Mr. Brougham frowned at her tone but continued his explanation. "When you didn't answer my knock, but there was still light in your room, I decided you couldn't be asleep. So, you'd gone to see someone. And that would have to be Phoebe Townley or your sister. I thought if I waited here I'd be sure to see you."

Lady Molly laughed, genuinely amused this time. "How long have you been lurking here? How absurd!"

She kissed him. Several minutes later Mr. Brougham raised his head. "But why were you crying?" he asked.

Lady Molly looked away and drew in her breath. "The most shocking thing," she said, not looking at him. "Kit, did you know? About my sister and Sir Marius?" She lowered her voice at the last words and glanced round her as if an eavesdropper might lurk among her painted ancestors.

"Yes. That is, I suspected something. And then I surprised them in an embrace this evening."

Lady Molly shuddered. "They are not discreet."

"Do you mind that much?" Mr. Brougham asked gently.

"Not about Sir Marius! You mustn't think that. But how *can* Juliana? Kit, I hardly know how to say this. When I was there just now, I heard—oh, Kit, Sir Marius is in Juliana's bedroom!"

Mr. Brougham knew better than to smile at Lady Molly's distress. But, elated by the final severance of Lady Molly's betrothal and the unusual opportunity to converse with her in private, he was unwise enough to defend Lady Rich.

"I think they are sincerely attached to each other," he said.

"But they have no right."

"I am only casually acquainted with your sister, Molly, but it seems clear to me that her marriage is little more than a charade."

"What does that matter? She's still bound to it. I suppose you'd like to see her run off with Sir Marius!"

"Yes, Molly, I would. Actually, I told Sir Marius so not two hours ago."

Lady Molly drew away from him. "You must be joking."

"No, I'm not." Mr. Brougham turned her to face him. "I can't speak for the lady's feelings, of course, but I can't help thinking she'd have a pleasanter life with Sir Marius than with her husband."

"Kit! How can you advocate a life of sin!"

"Be reasonable, Molly. Eloping to the Continent with Sir Marius won't make her sin any worse, really. Quite the contrary: Lord Rich would no doubt divorce her as soon as possible. Then he could remarry and beget that heir he wants so desperately. And I have no doubt that your sister would have no trouble persuading Sir Marius to marry her."

"You would approve of such behaviour? You've encouraged it?"

"Molly, you're overwrought," said Mr. Brougham, only now understanding that Lady Molly was completely serious. He drew a handkerchief from his pocket. Putting his hand under her chin, he tilted her face upwards, intending to dry her tears. Lady Molly pulled away.

"Don't touch me!"

Mr. Brougham dropped his hands and took a step back. The moonlight had disappeared; he could see little but

115

shadows where Lady Molly stood. He gave a low whistle. "You are angry, aren't you? Poor Molly. It must have been a shock."

Lady Molly spoke with precision, spitting the words out from between her teeth. "It is your conduct that shocks me. I am profoundly shocked that you can regard with levity—that you can *encourage*—the ruining of my sister's life."

Mr. Brougham ran a hand through his dark curls. "All right, Molly. In society's eyes she'd be ruined for life, but would you please try to look at her from her point of view? From the point of view of her own happiness? They'd have quite enough money to live in comfort. And it's not as if she had any children."

"But she has a duty to her husband. Don't you believe that, Kit?"

"I understand your objection; it's just not one I subscribe to. She's not been a dutiful wife all these years, Molly. Rich would no doubt be glad to see her go. He'd brave the scandal for the prospect of a new wife and an heir. Why shouldn't the marriage be dissolved?"

"Is that your idea of marriage? That it can be dissolved at a whim?"

"Molly, may I remind you that we are discussing an entirely hypothetical situation? As far as I know, Sir Marius and Lady Rich may have no intention of acting on my suggestion."

"That's not the point. You made the suggestion. I find this revelation of your beliefs disgusting."

Mr. Brougham looked at Lady Molly, a shadowy figure with her hair hanging loose about her shoulders. "Molly, Molly, are you by any chance about to say you can't marry me?"

Goaded by the laughter in his voice, Lady Molly could only say, "Yes! That's precisely what I want to tell you!"

The moon had broken free from the obscuring clouds and Mr. Brougham could see Lady Molly's face. There were dark circles under her eyes and her lower lip trembled.

"You'll marry me," said Mr. Brougham. He pulled her into a harsh embrace, and neither of them spoke for a long time.

The moonlight faded. When Mr. Brougham relinquished Lady Molly, the darkness was almost complete.

"Well, Molly," said Mr. Brougham, a smile playing about his lips, "you'll marry me, won't you?" Then he added, injudiciously (the brandy he had consumed that evening had impaired his judgment), "Your scruples are so nice, my dear! Why can't you sympathise with your sister a little? Wouldn't you still kiss me even if you had married Sir Marius all those years ago?"

Lady Molly wrenched herself from his arms. "You are offensive, Mr. Brougham!"

She ran down the hall. When she had reached the far staircase she turned and looked back at Mr. Brougham, who had not moved.

"I cannot marry someone who considers the vows of matrimony so unimportant," she told him, and fled.

Mr. Brougham stood in the gallery for some time after Lady Molly had left. The choke in her voice as she made her declaration had not escaped him. He finished the decanter of the Duke's excellent cognac before he went to sleep, but he was far less unhappy than Lady Molly, who sobbed into her pillow until the small hours of the morning.

When Lady Molly awoke the next morning with a throbbing headache, she reconsidered her scheme of confronting Lady Rich. Lady Molly felt she never wanted to speak to anyone again, and that Lady Rich was preceded only by Mr. Brougham on the list of people she would actively avoid. Then it occurred to her that, if she had not dreamed her horrid encounter of the night before with Mr. Brougham, it was possible that Lady Rich had fled Seekings Castle. At that thought, without pausing to examine her motives, Lady Molly leapt out of bed, rang for her maid, and was in the breakfast room in less than twenty minutes.

The ormolu clock on the mantel struck nine as she entered the breakfast room.

Mrs. Townley was the only occupant of the sun-filled room.

"Good-morning, Molly! You've just missed all the gentlemen. It is, they tell me, a perfect day for shooting."

Lady Molly glanced out a window for the first time that morning. "Why, it's glorious out."

"You sound surprised! It's been glorious all week. If we weren't so frantic with rehearsals, I'd suggest another skating party."

"No, not another skating party."

Lady Molly poured herself a cup of coffee and sank into a chair.

"There are freshly baked biscuits, Lady Mary," Newcome, who had followed her into the breakfast room, remonstrated. "Or some fruit?"

Lady Molly permitted the butler to serve her a bowl of strawberries from Seekings's renowned forcing house, but her uncharacteristic lethargy was noticed by both Newcome and Mrs. Townley. They were vouchsafed a clue as to the cause of her distress when she asked Newcome, in a voice that shook, if Lady Rich had risen yet.

Newcome informed her that Lady Rich's breakfast in bed was not even due to be brought up for another hour. His low opinion of the question was implicit in his tone.

"I see," said Lady Molly. "Of course she won't be up yet. Foolish of me. You may go, Newcome."

When the door had shut behind the butler, Mrs. Townley turned to her friend.

"What was that about?" she demanded. Why do you want Juliana? And you look quite hag-ridden! Did you sleep badly?"

"Phoebe, I'm so confused," confessed Lady Molly, staring into her coffee cup as if it might hold an oracular answer to her problems.

"Do tell me what's wrong, Molly. I've hardly spoken to you since I arrived, except about the play."

Lady Molly roused herself at this. "I'm sorry, Phoebe. I've neglected you dreadfully. Forgive me? And I'll tell you precisely what is on my mind, if you won't be bored."

"My dear, I am all agog. And do start at the beginning! I've been so curious about your reunion with Sir Marius."

Lady Molly bit her lip. "Gracious, I haven't talked to you! This will be a long story."

Fortunately, the two ladies were undisturbed for the next hour. Lady Molly poured into Mrs. Townley's ear the whole story of what she termed her "entanglement" with Mr. Brougham. Mrs. Townley, who was highly amused by the tale, did not scruple to express her opinion to Lady Molly. Not only was Mr. Brougham both wealthier and of higher birth than Sir Marius, Mrs. Townley told her friend, but he was also blessed with far more moral probity.

"But that's not saying much!" riposted Lady Molly. "I agree, one cannot imagine Mr. Brougham conducting an *affaire* under the nose of his *fiancée*—such bad *ton,* he seems to think—"

Mrs. Townley interrupted Lady Molly. "That's not fair. From what you say, it does not seem as if Mr. Brougham took that aspect of Sir Marius's misconduct so lightly. He surely didn't mean that he approved of Sir Marius's conduct."

"Oh, no, he simply encouraged him to continue in it," said Lady Molly, her voice dripping with sarcasm.

"There's quite a difference," said Mrs. Townley. "Mr. Brougham sounds to me to have simply a sensible view of the situation."

"Phoebe, you can't think so!"

"I can and I do," said Mrs. Townley staunchly. "I hope

you won't be angry with me, Molly, but you did ask my opinion."

Lady Molly smiled. She was immensely relieved to have confided in someone, although Mrs. Townley's calm demeanour in the face of what Lady Molly considered a scandalous story was disconcerting. "I promise I won't be angry. You think I was wrong?"

"You'd had a bad shock. And your *fiancé* has treated you abominably," Mrs. Townley began.

"But you do think I was wrong? I promise I shan't mind you saying so!"

"Well, then, yes, yes, I do. I think you should marry Mr. Brougham, and I suspect you will find his attitude towards marriage—other people's, that is—quite common. Your own marriage would be nothing like that of your sister, don't you see?"

Lady Molly pushed away her coffee cup, put her elbows on the table, and propped her chin in her hand. "I'm interested to hear you say that, Phoebe. Will you be angry if I say that you are the last person I should expect to utter such sentiments?"

"Because of my husband?" Mrs. Townley said. "I see what you mean."

"I can imagine nothing worse than what you went through," said Lady Molly. "And I only knew the merest fraction of it."

"It was painful, yes, and continues to be. But my husband's infidelity did not destroy me, Molly. I should think I am happier, on the whole, than your sister. I may yet reconcile myself to Arthur, but for now I am enjoying the time back with my family. And, Molly, make no mistake: I do not for an instant regret marrying him."

Lady Molly had only once before dared speak so openly with Mrs. Townley about her husband's notorious pursuit —and capture—of Lady Cowper. She had pictured her friend as a martyred saint and had hardly been able to greet Arthur Townley with civility when she encountered him in London. She stared as she listened to her friend explain that the happy days of their married life had been worth the humiliation that followed. Mrs. Townley told Lady Molly that, regardless of his conduct, she still loved Arthur Townley.

Lady Molly had never considered the possibility that Mrs. Townley might return to her errant husband. Long after their *tête-à-tête* had been interrupted by the Fancot sisters, Lady Molly was still musing on what Mrs. Townley had said.

Mrs. Townley refused to hazard a guess as to whether Lady Rich would elope with Sir Marius. "For even Mr. Brougham said it was merely a suggestion," she pointed out to Lady Molly. "You have no reason for assuming that your sister will act on it. Indeed, however enthusiastic Sir Marius may have been when the idea was propounded to him last night, he may by this morning have changed his mind about so momentous an undertaking. My experience has been that gentlemen very often regret—or even forget—what they have said in their cups."

Her matter-of-fact attitude cheered Lady Molly. "Thank heaven he released me from our betrothal in writing! It would be dreadful if he were so inebriated as to forget that we're no longer to be married," she replied.

When ten o'clock had come and gone without any domestic upheaval, Lady Molly knew that Lady Rich must have been in her room to receive her breakfast in bed. Lady Molly's vision of a midnight decampment dissolved. Enormously relieved, she rang to have her horse saddled. By eleven o'clock she was galloping across the Seekings park, a groom following at a discreet distance.

There was not as yet much snow on the ground, and Lady Molly rode as fast as she dared. With the wind whipping her hair out from under her riding hat, Lady Molly forgot all the problems waiting for her at the castle. She urged her mare onward, only finally reining her in when they had reached the high ridge that overlooked the shooting ground.

For once, Mr. Brougham had joined the shooting party. So poor a shot was he, however, that at a break he ceded his place to the late-rising Conte di Innamorati and strolled round to Lord St. Omar's position. Lord St. Omar, by far the champion marksman in the house party, cordially accepted Mr. Brougham's request to observe him for a while. Mr. Brougham's shooting might be disgraceful, but he was a neck-or-nothing horseman and a member of the Four-Horse Club. Lord St. Omar considered the F.H.C.'s diversion of one monthly drive to Salt Hill sadly flat (and its distinctive costume of a spotted necktie and a striped waistcoat deplorably loud), but he allowed that membership in that exclusive group could excuse a poor showing in any other field of sport. So he welcomed Mr. Brougham and did not comment on Mr. Brougham's abandonment of the field. After the first round, embarrassed by Mr. Brougham's praise, he seized on a distraction and pointed out his sister, on her grey mare, silhouetted against the sky.

Lady Molly held her mare still, waiting for the groom to catch up with her and trying to identify the gentlemen shooting below. She could not know that Mr. Brougham was looking up at her, but when, after a few minutes, she remembered that he had not been at breakfast and thus might well have risen early and joined the shooting party, she turned her horse round and cantered back to meet her groom. She took one last look over her shoulder before the shooting party was hidden from view, but the gentlemen were indistinguishable in their tweeds, and she could not find even her own father and brother.

The ride had heartened her. She changed her mind once again and decided that she had to speak to her sister. Lady Rich ought to be told how little Sir Marius meant to Lady Molly, if only for the sake of Lady Molly's pride. Lady Molly envisioned a triumphant encounter, she would tell Juliana that her behaviour was disgraceful, then assure her that she was welcome to Sir Marius. Lady Molly forgot that her sister was a keen observer and might be expected to have noticed the understanding between Mr. Brougham and Sir Marius's *fiancée*. Lady Molly ascertained from Newcome (who was beginning to realise something was in the wind) that Lady Rich had not yet left her bedchamber. The walk to Lady Rich's bedchamber seemed much shorter by daylight. When Lady Molly entered, Lady Rich dismissed her maid.

"For I can see by your very expression that you want to talk to me in private, Molly! What is it?"

Lady Molly, still standing, looked at her exasperating sister. Lady Rich was fully clothed, unusual at noon, and seemed to be writing a letter.

Lady Molly realised that it would be far easier, if less romantic, to elope by daylight.

"Are you running off with Sir Marius?" she said.

"Always so forthright! Do sit down, Molly."

"But are you? I do think you ought to tell me."

Lady Rich did not respond.

"You are. I'm sure of it."

"Why?" asked Lady Rich.

"Is that a letter from Father, or your husband, or me?" countered Lady Molly.

Lady Rich laughed. "You, but I've only written the first sentence. I didn't know how much you knew."

"I know you've been carrying on an illicit liaison with my *fiancé*. Not that he is my *fiancé* any longer."

"How did you find out?" asked Lady Rich. "Did Kit Brougham tell you?"

"No, I guessed. And then I came here late last night to talk to you and heard voices."

"Were you dreadfully shocked?" asked Lady Rich, not looking at her sister. "I'm sorry. I wouldn't have done anything, you know, had your affections been engaged with Sir Marius. I promise you that, Molly."

Lady Molly believed her sister and was, somehow, no longer angry. "I suppose this is partly my fault," she said. "I can't approve of your behaviour, Juliana, but that's your affair. And I should have broken off the betrothal weeks ago. Or never have agreed to marry him in the first place."

"You were very young," said Lady Rich. After a few minutes of silence, she added, "As was I when I married Rich."

Their eyes met for the first time since Lady Molly had entered the room. Lady Molly smiled and shrugged her shoulders.

"What a silly tangle! And how fortunate I knew the moment I saw him again that I didn't wish to marry him. But, Juliana, do you truly care for him?"

"It's not impossible, my dear! I know you've found other interests, but Sir Marius remains a highly personable gentleman! He's good-natured and everyone likes him—a change, I might say, from Lord Rich—and he's recently come into a comfortable fortune. He never quarrels, and he loves to dance. I find him very attractive, and he has become unalterably devoted to me."

Lady Molly sighed. "If you're to leave England with him, I sincerely hope his devotion does not alter."

She rose from her chair, crossed the room, and stood before Lady Rich. "Juliana, have you truly considered? How can you do this?"

"I know, I know. It will break Aunt Amelia's heart," said Lady Rich, her lips twisted into a slight smile.

"It will," said Lady Molly.

"But not yours. Or Father's, or Jamie's. And I promise you my husband will be pleased to be rid of me. I'm very expensive, you know."

"Juliana, you're not serious. He couldn't wish for the scandal."

"I am perfectly serious. He will have all the glory of the injured party. Think of William Lamb. He's far better liked than ever, poor dear, after the way Caro behaved."

Lady Caroline Lamb's pursuit of Lord Byron had been the greatest *on-dit* of London in the spring of Lady Molly's come-out, and she knew Lady Rich was right. Lord Rich's position would not suffer for his wife's misdeeds. People might say that William Lamb's political career was blighted, but he was still welcome everywhere. Indeed, any ill feeling towards him was due to his reconciliation with Lady Caroline rather than to their earlier separation.

"But you'll never be able to return to England," said Lady Molly. "Shan't you miss home, living in those dismal Continental spas?"

"I'm not thinking of settling in Vichy. Or even Baden-Baden. We'll go to Paris, or Vienna. Paris, I should think. And, in any case, it will only be for a few years. Sir Marius and I shall be married as soon as Lord Rich gets a divorce bill through the Lords, which I make no doubt he will do with all celerity. And he'll remarry some poor young *débutante,* and I will return to England a married woman. Look at Lady Holland! I shan't be able to return to Almack's, but that doesn't disturb me a whit. I'll be back in London and holding 'at homes' again within two years. And Rich will have a dreadfully ugly little squalling heir. Will you cut my acquaintance?"

Lady Rich extended her hand to her sister. Lady Molly smiled and clasped her sister's hand.

"I cannot like it, Juliana, but I shan't cut you. And of

course my attitude will be what the *ton* looks at, since it was I who had my future husband stolen. You're right—the scandal will blow over. And Mrs. Drummond Burrell will never darken your door again!"

"Such an odious woman!" said Lady Rich. "And no one will feel too much pity for you, you know, when you're happily married to a much more eligible *parti.*"

Lady Molly flushed and snatched her hand away. "That's by no means certain, Juliana. I'm quite on the shelf by now."

Lady Rich was watching her sister carefully. "You've quarrelled with Mr. Brougham," she announced. "Foolish of you."

"How dare you tell me I'm behaving foolishly?" demanded Lady Molly, but without any heat in her words. She knew too well that, having forgiven her sister, she had no reason to not forgive Mr. Brougham.

"His attentions will spare you from too many condolences on Sir Marius's disappearance. I had relied on that," said Lady Rich.

"Juliana, it is none of your concern. I'm not trying to dissuade you from a course of action I can only think of as wicked—"

"Wisely, darling, because you wouldn't have the least success and you might make me angry," Lady Rich interrupted.

"—So would you please leave me alone to conduct my life in my own way."

"Of course," said Lady Rich. "But it's much more pleasant to face the whispers of the *ton* with a gentleman at your side."

Lady Molly raised her chin. "I am a Drayton," she said. "I don't care two bits what any of them say!"

"Precisely my feelings, Molly!" said Lady Rich, and Lady Molly had to laugh.

"Now I shan't say anything more except that Mr. Brougham admires you very much," Lady Rich concluded.

"I have to go. Sir Marius and I are going out for a drive. Only you know that we shan't return. I've assumed you'll send my things after me. There's only room for a few bandboxes in the curricle."

"You're eloping in a curricle!"

"Just as far as London. I do hope it doesn't snow this afternoon. Then we'll take Rich's travelling chaise to Dover and sail for France."

"You're quite unprincipled, Juliana. Do you know that? Stealing your husband's chaise to elope with another man!"

"Not stealing, Molly. It's much too ugly to take over to France. But Elise had already taken down my boxes and I really must go."

"Is Sir Marius waiting for you downstairs?" asked Lady Molly. "If you wouldn't mind, could I go down with you? Somehow I feel I ought to assure him that I don't mind. I cede all my rights to you, or something of that sort."

Lady Rich had no objection, and her sister accompanied her downstairs. Sir Marius was waiting for her in the great hall. He was perceptibly nervous, flicking his whip against his left hand as he paced the floor. When he saw Lady Rich's companion, his jaw dropped. With an effort, he walked to the foot of the stairs and wished both ladies a good morning.

"I was just to take your sister for a ride, Lady Molly," he said. "But if you wish to speak to me . . . ?" He tugged at his cravat.

Lady Rich glanced round the great hall. Seeing no one, she laid her hand on Sir Marius's arm. "It's all right, my dear," she said. "She knows."

Sir Marius looked at Lady Molly. He gulped. "I, er, owe you an apology, Lady Molly. I can't think what to say, but that, um, I—was Brougham correct? You do wish to break off our engagement?"

Lady Molly laughed. "If I didn't before, I certainly

should now! You may take Juliana with a clear conscience." She paused, realising what she had said, and blushed. "That is, as far as I'm concerned," she amended. "And let's take the apology as said, shall we?"

Sir Marius met her eyes. "You were a very sweet eighteen-year-old," he said. "I was truly fond of you."

"I've wondered," said Lady Molly. "I'm glad to hear that. Now go, both of you!"

Newcome (who had finally discovered what was in the wind) seemed to materialize from nowhere to open the great double doors for Lady Rich and Sir Marius. A groom was holding Sir Marius's bays just outside. Lady Molly stayed where she was, four steps up on the great staircase, and she could see across the great hall to the carriage-way. She watched as Sir Marius helped her sister up into the curricle and leapt up himself. He took the reins and dismissed the groom. The bandboxes, Lady Molly noted, must be hidden under the fur rug that she could discern on the floor of the curricle. Sir Marius clucked to the horses. Just before they drove away, Lady Rich turned and blew a kiss to her sister. Newcome shut the doors.

Walking back up the stairs, Lady Molly wondered how she ought to break the news to her father and the rest of the house party. She stopped short at the landing, in front of the great Caravaggio that was her father's favourite painting. She cursed aloud. Newcome had disappeared again. There was fortunately no one to hear Lady Molly exclaim, "What the devil am I to do about the play!"

Chapter Fifteen

Upon reflection, Lady Molly decided that her father must be consulted before she mentioned what had happened to anyone, even Mrs. Townley. She spent the afternoon in her room. Newcome had instructions to inform her as soon as the shooting party returned, but the footman whom he sent on this errand was met at the door by Lady Molly's abigail, who told him that Lady Molly had fallen asleep and should not be disturbed. In consequence, it was not until half-past seven that Lady Molly, awakened by her abigail to dress for dinner, was able to speak to her father.

He was dressed and reading a book by his fire. Lady Molly, hardly waiting for his valet to leave the room, announced to him that Lady Rich had fled. The Duke took the news with equanimity. He said that he had long predicted such an eventuality, and he asked Lady Molly how much she minded Sir Marius's defection. When she assured him that the loss of Sir Marius was the least painful circumstance of Juliana's flight, the Duke observed that he must send a notice of their betrothal's termination to the *Morning Post* immediately.

"How will you let people know what Juliana's done?" Lady Molly asked.

"That sort of news travels fast. I shouldn't be surprised if Rich hears it before he lands in England. But I shall make an announcement at dinner tonight. That would seem to be the least troublesome way to let our guests know."

"Father, is that all you have to say? Juliana's ruined herself!"

"Her conduct is deplorable. But you probably don't know that Juliana's conduct has always been deplorable. And, really, I don't see how cutting her off without a shilling or blotting her name from the family Bible will serve matters."

"You're so calm!" Lady Molly said incredulously. "Would you behave like this had it been I?"

"You're not married; you're not eight-and-twenty; and you would never so disgrace yourself," said the Duke. "Molly, I don't wish to talk further about Juliana—and we have little time before dinner, anyway."

The Duke of Chettam was an indulgent father, but it never occurred to Lady Molly that she might press a subject her father had expressly dismissed.

"But there's something else, Father," she said as he rose. "What should I do about the play? I'll have to let all those who planned to attend know that it's cancelled. What should I say?"

"I don't like that," said the Duke, thinking about it. "Far better to hold the play and the ball as originally planned."

"Do we dare?" breathed Lady Molly. "But that would be shocking."

"So's what Juliana's done. And if we want her ever to be received in English society again—which I assume you

132

do—we ought to put a brave face on it. And the play's splendid. I don't see why we should let Juliana's caprices spoil Christmas."

"We might be able to hold the ball, but we simply can't have the play," said Lady Molly. "You forget, Father, that Juliana and Sir Marius had our leading *rôles*."

"Pity that. I'd forgotten. That makes it so much more difficult to make it seem we countenance Juliana's behaviour."

"But we don't. I mean, everyone will have to know we didn't *want* her to do this."

"Yes, but they don't need to know quite how selfish of her it was. Can't the play be salvaged? Calling in new actors?"

"Short of hiring a few from Drury Lane, we can't save the play."

"Hire some from Drury Lane, then."

Father! In three days, they're to be found, brought back from London, and taught a new part! At Christmastime! It can't be done."

The Duke had lost interest in the subject. "It can't be done, then," he said. "Let's join our guests in the drawing room. And we must converse on an unexceptionable topic until I have a chance to tell everyone. The book I'm reading is quite delightful," the Duke said as he ushered her out the door. "Brougham gave it to me. Apparently he's acquainted with the author. A Mr. Peacock, who Brougham says is in the most straitened circumstances."

Lady Molly knew what was expected of her. As they strolled down the corridor, she gave a sigh of resignation, pushed to the back of her mind all thoughts of the impending scandal and asked her father what the book was about.

"Not very much," said the Duke. "A satire. But there is the most amusing portrait of poor Tom Moore. I promised Brougham I'd see if something could be done for this Mr. Peacock. A place at the East India Company, perhaps. I like Brougham, you know. He's a clever young man. I can't imagine he gets along well with old Annesley. You haven't met Annesley, have you? The stuffiest man in England. I wasn't surprised to hear ' he'd turned Evangelical. He's in abominable health, which may explain the religion. Not much older than I, but they say he's on his last legs."

Luckily for Lady Molly's peace of mind, they were joined at this point by the Conte and Contessa and conversation was general for the rest of the descent.

The Duke's brief announcement that Lady Rich and Sir Marius had left Seekings, bound for France, was received with even more horror than Lady Molly had expected. Lady Amelia excused herself from the table and Lord St. Omar, at a gesture from his father, followed to comfort his aunt. Lady Wellburn seemed delighted at the chance to denounce the morals of the younger generation. Lady Molly let her eyes meet Mr. Brougham's for an infinitesimal instant. But most of the house party were appalled at Lady Rich and Sir Marius's disregard for the play.

"We worked so hard!" exclaimed Tony Laverham. "How could they!"

The Duke had said nothing about the fate of *The Procrastinator* and Lady Molly was besieged with questions. She could not take as firm a stand about cancelling the play as she wished; she was touched by how much her guests seemed to care about the play. She had spent the better part of the preceding month working these people far harder than most of them had ever worked before. She had reflected many times that she would be fortunate if even Phoebe Townley and Lord St. Omar, continued to speak to her after the play, so harsh had she been with her cast. But it seemed that they understood why she had worked them so hard. Lady Molly felt a lump in her throat and her lower lip trembled slightly. She told them that if they could think of any possible way to stage the play without the hero and heroine, she would be glad to hear it. She added that the ball on Christmas Eve would go forward as planned.

These announcements over, ordinary dinner-table etiquette returned. Each person spoke to his left-hand neighbour. Lady Molly had been taken in to dinner by the Conte, who, almost alone among the guests, had no interest in the play, and so she was spared further discussion of the catastrophe until the table turned. Then Lord Dewhurst fell to her lot. She managed to snub him, but Lady Molly steeled herself for discussion of *The Procrastinator* after dinner.

She was not mistaken. Mrs. Townley had been seated between Lord St. Omar and Mr. Laverham at dinner and she had not wasted her time. Lord St. Omar and Lady Amelia had returned to the table by the time the soup was removed. He and Mrs. Townley had conversed intently until Lady Molly (Lady Amelia clearly being incapable of performing the normal duties of a hostess) had caught her eye and risen to withdraw. Mrs. Townley had not spoken to Lady Molly while the ladies were alone, but as soon as the gentlemen joined them, Mrs. Townley told Lady Molly she had something to tell her.

"Lord St. Omar and I have the most famous scheme," Mrs. Townley said. "You did say you'd like anything that saved the play."

"That's not precisely what I said," demurred Lady Molly.

"But you would like to put on the play, wouldn't you?"

"Yes, I suppose," Lady Molly replied warily. "What do you have in mind?"

Mr. Laverham came up to the two ladies. "Couldn't we go after them?" he suggested. "Bring them back. You could tell them you wouldn't mind them absconding once

Christmas was over. I remember when my cousin eloped, my uncle went after her."

Lord St. Omar and Mr. Brougham had also drifted towards the ladies. Lady Molly shared a smile at Mr. Laverham's reminiscence with Mr. Brougham and was furious with herself. Lord St. Omar directed a quelling glance at Tony Laverham.

"It's not as if my sister were sixteen and running off to Gretna Green! Rich could follow her, if he were here and if he chose to. I'm certainly not going to set off to drag two grown people back to Seekings! I doubt either I or my father have any legal right to do so."

Lady Molly laughed. "And I'm sure Father wouldn't ride off *ventre-à-terre* to reclaim Juliana. But what's your famous scheme, Phoebe?"

Mrs. Townley paused for a minute. She looked round at the small group, all waiting for her to speak. "First tell me, Molly, do you truly intend to hold the ball?"

"Yes, the ball will take place."

"People will say it's frightfully improper," Mrs. Townley warned.

Lady Molly said, *"Tant pis,"* at the same moment her brother said, "Who cares?"

Mrs. Townley laughed. "Such it is to be a Drayton. So you wouldn't mind the talk. And it is a shame that Lady Rich's caprice should rob us of the play."

Lady Molly choked slightly to hear her sister's flight described as a caprice, but she nodded.

"What *are* you getting at, Phoebe?"

Lord St. Omar spoke before Mrs. Townley could reply. "And a new Templeton Blaine comes along only once in a few years. It's an important event in literary history."

This time Mr. Brougham choked. Tony Laverham could stand the suspense no longer. "Tell us your plan!" he burst out. "We all agree the play should go on if at all possible."

"Well then," said Mrs. Townley. "You'll help me convince Lady Molly to cooperate."

"Oh, no," said Lady Molly.

"You know Arabella's lines, don't you?"

"I collect you refer to Lady Rich's?" said Lady Molly.

"She's forfeited them," said Mrs. Townley. "You'll have the honor of first presenting them to the world."

"I couldn't possibly," said Lady Molly.

"But you do know the lines?" said Lord St. Omar.

"Oh, yes, I know the lines, but what good does that do when I can't act and when we don't have the procrastinator himself?" Lady Molly demanded, but she knew her fate was sealed.

Mr. Brougham was smiling broadly when Lord St. Omar and Mrs. Townley turned to look at him. He raised a hand to forestall them from speaking. "Yes, I admit, I know most of the lines."

"How fortunate that you have attended so many rehearsals!" said Mrs. Townley. "Quite providential!"

"However, my Evangelical principles forbid me to take part," Mr. Brougham continued imperturbably.

"Fiddlesticks!" said Mrs. Townley.

"I thought it was your uncle's Evangelical principles," said Lord St. Omar.

"Your Evangelical principles didn't stop you from attending rehearsals," said the Contessa di Innamorati, who had realised what was under discussion and joined the group.

"You must," said Tony Laverham. "God, if I've memorised all those lines for nothing! Oh, I beg your pardon, ladies."

Mr. Brougham did not reply. Tony Laverham looked as if he were about to explode. Lady Molly decided it was time for her to intervene.

"He's dying to do it. Just look at him," she announced. "And I wager he'll be good, too. I give you all fair warning that I shan't be more than passable. But you'll do it, won't you, Mr. Brougham?"

Mr. Brougham laughed. "You're correct, as usual, Lady Molly. I confess I shall enjoy trying my hand at acting. And let us just hope no one tells Lord Annesley."

"You could always tell him you succumbed under great pressure and for the most chivalrous of motives," Mrs. Townley consoled him.

"And you'll be properly penitential by the time this is over," said Lord St. Omar. "I don't think you'll enjoy the next few days."

"Do I detect a mutiny?" asked Lady Molly. "A rebellious spirit among my subordinates?"

"Exactly," said Lord St. Omar. "Mrs. Townley and I will take over from here, or you'll never learn all the lines and staging. We have only two days, remember."

Lady Molly closed her eyes in horror. "I can't believe I said I'd do this."

"I'll help you with your lines," said Mr. Laverham. "We have lots of scenes together and I know all mine."

Mrs. Townley told him to leave Lady Molly alone. "The most important thing is for both of you to get to sleep," she said to Mr. Brougham and Lady Molly.

"But it's half-past ten!" Mr. Brougham protested.

"Yes, but then we can begin rehearsing you two at nine," said Lord St. Omar.

Mr. Brougham groaned and informed Lord St. Omar that he had never before thought him a vengeful man. But Mr. Brougham's brandy consumption of the night before had left its ravages on his face, and Lord St. Omar was firm in his insistence that Mr. Brougham needed a long night's sleep before facing the rigours of rehearsal. Mrs. Townley was no less determined that Lady Molly needed to rest. Lord St. Omar and Mrs. Townley, well pleased with their evening's work, shepherded their charges to bed, adjuring them that this might be their last chance to sleep until Christmas was over.

Chapter Sixteen

In later years, Lady Molly never thought of the two days preceding that Christmas without a shudder. All she wanted was to speak alone with Mr. Brougham. And though she was forced to stand opposite him on a stage for nine hours a day, the two of them were not alone for a minute.

Nor did Mr. Brougham seem eager to speak to her. He was absorbed in his _rôle,_ propping his lines up before him as they ate a cold nuncheon, and never talking of anything but the play. After weeks of such intimacy, Lady Molly was chilled. Lady Molly, the originator of the scheme, found herself hating _The Procrastinator._

Matters were not improved by Mr. Brougham's un-doubted talent. He learned his lines far faster than she did, which galled Lady Molly, and he promised to be an improvement over Sir Marius, who had never been more than adequate in the part. Lady Molly knew that she was not an improvement over Lady Rich. She felt herself to be the only weak member of a sparkling cast and was close to tears by the time they had run through the entire play twice.

Happy to escape, the minor actors fled from the lesser ballroom as soon as the second run-through was over. At her brother's request, Lady Molly stayed behind, as did Mr. Brougham and Mrs. Townley.

"I know, I know, Jamie," she said before he could speak. "I did warn you that I shouldn't be more than passable. But please don't make us rehearse anything again. It won't help. And I'm so tired."

"Only the two scenes alone with you two," said Lord St. Omar. "Those are the only ones that really need work."

"You're far more than passable, Lady Molly," Mr. Brougham interjected. The conviction in his voice was absolute, and all three of his auditors were surprised at his confidence. "You have a lovely speaking voice; you move well on stage; and your scenes with Tony Laverham are genuinely amusing. Arabella's an unsuccessful character anyway. Blaine hasn't put her down precisely as an *ingénue* or as a schemer: he doesn't seem to have made up his mind. In terms of the plot, she can't be very clever. One must assume Arabella's successful machinations are by chance. You're doing quite well with the material at hand. Just continue to play her as giddy and thoughtless and you should be all right."

Everyone stared at Mr. Brougham. He blushed slightly. "That's what I think, anyway," he said apologetically. "Oh, and we haven't rehearsed the songs yet. Those will be easy for you. You've a much finer voice than Lady Rich."

"That's true," said Mrs. Townley. "Molly, your singing is always in demand. So it won't matter how much trouble you have with the play itself. The *entr'acte* will work and that will please the audience. And Mr. Brougham's right:

you're not bad at all. Better than I expected, to be honest."

Lady Molly and Lord St. Omar were still staring at Mr. Brougham. Rattled by their steady gaze, he coughed and suggested that they begin rehearsing the two scenes that Lord St. Omar had suggested.

The scenes did go better this third time. Mr. Brougham and Lady Molly were still unaccountably ill at ease with each other, touching each other gingerly and addressing lines more frequently to the audience than to each other. But Lady Molly, heartened by Mr. Brougham's praise, acted much more convincingly than before. Mr. Brougham was, as before, very funny. He once even drew a laugh from Lady Molly, who had heard every joke in *The Procrastinator* a hundred times. Lord St. Omar, who had not caught the joke, frowned slightly. He wondered what it was that had made Lady Molly laugh, but he did not want to break the scene to enquire.

"Very good!" he said when they had finished. "We can go to tea with a clear conscience."

Lady Molly walked over to the pianoforte that stood at the side of the stage. She flipped through the music on the rack. "Can't we go over the songs once before tea?" she asked. "I should feel so much more comfortable."

"I thought you were so tired!" said Lord St. Omar.

Mrs. Townley, seated next to Lord St. Omar in the first row of chairs, put her hand on his arm. "She wants to do what she's good at now," Mrs. Townley told Lord St. Omar in a stage whisper. "Poor dear, we must indulge her. And applaud very loudly."

Lady Molly cast a fulminating glance at Mrs. Townley. "I merely wish to assume myself that we will be able to perform the *entr'acte* as well," she said with dignity.

"You wish me to play?" asked Mr. Brougham, who was still standing in the middle of the stage.

"Yes, but I'll also expect you to sing," said Lady Molly. "These are duets."

Mr. Brougham nodded, walked off the stage, and sat down at the pianoforte. "Which of the three shall we start with?"

" 'Had We Never' is the longest," said Lady Molly. "Let's get it over with."

Very well," said Mr. Brougham. "Just let me look at the music."

He picked out the melody with one hand, added a few tentative chords, enquired as to whether the key would suit Lady Molly, and began to play.

Lady Molly sang the first few lines, then stopped. "But you're not singing! You must!"

Mr. Brougham sighed and began again. This time he sang along and they made it through the first verse of the ballad without incident. But they were no more than two measures into the second verse when Lady Molly began to laugh.

Mr. Brougham stopped playing. "Is my singing so bad, then?"

Lady Molly looked round the lesser ballroom. Mrs. Townley and Lord St. Omar were their only auditors. "Oh, do cut line, Kit!" she said. "I'm most impressed!"

"I beg your pardon?" said Mr. Brougham, rising from the piano bench. He too was beginning to laugh.

"What is it, Molly?" asked Lord St. Omar.

Lady Molly didn't look at her brother. She looked directly at Mr. Brougham. "How could I not have seen! Of course. You are Templeton Blaine."

Lord St. Omar and Mrs. Townley exchanged astonished glances.

Mr. Brougham, oblivious of their presence, took Lady Molly's hands in his. "You're quite right," he said. "I gave myself away with the song?"

"Yes, just as I thought you might. We cut out that second verse, don't you remember? Back at the very beginning of rehearsals. You shouldn't have known it at all."

142

"I see! Of course! And it was my little speech on why Arabella was Blaine's greatest failure that first tipped you off?"

"Yes. And, you know, she's not a great failure. A bit wooden, I grant you, but the play's still wonderful. By far your best yet—and they've all been very good!"

"I'm glad you like them," said Mr. Brougham earnestly.

"I do. I like them tremendously. And so that's why you wanted to meet me in London—and why you wanted to come down here for Christmas."

Mr. Brougham phrased his response carefully. "Although the circumstances of our first meeting are as you have stated, what happened then was completely unexpected."

Lady Molly looked up at him, her brows furrowed, unsure of his meaning.

Mr. Brougham tried again to explain, less formally this time. "I was tipped a leveller when I heard you'd bought my script from that scoundrel Costigan. But there was nothing I could do, so I determined to get myself invited to Seekings. I wanted to at least be able to watch the mutilation of my play by a group of amateurs."

"How angry you must have been!" said Lady Molly.

Mr. Brougham grinned. "I was," he admitted. "But you're doing just as well as Drury Lane. And I've had far more say in the rehearsals than they ever allowed me there."

"You knew it was I who had bought the script," said Lady Molly, trying to remember what he had said when he was first presented to her.

"Yes. I begged Lady Rich to present me to you because I wanted to meet the unscrupulous young lady whom I had been cursing for days."

"I see. I would never have guessed you were so angry."

"That's because I was tipped another leveller when I met you," said Mr. Brougham.

The boxing cant did not disguise what he meant, and

Mrs. Townley tried to push Lord St. Omar out of the room. But Mr. Brougham turned his head away from Lady Molly when they rose.

"Lord St. Omar, Mrs. Townley," he called. "You will respect my secret?"

They both nodded. Now that the delicate moment had been broken (although Mr. Brougham still retained Lady Molly's hands), Mrs. Townley felt she could ask a question. "But why does it have to be a secret?"

"None of you seemed to believe me, but I was quite serious about my uncle's Evangelical principles. He won't mind one performance in amateur theatricals, but I honestly believe he'd cut me out of his will if he knew I were writing plays for Drury Lane. The estate's entailed, of course, but I shouldn't enjoy trying to keep up Annesley without any money."

"Besides, it must have been exciting to see if your plays could be successful without trading on your name and position," said Lady Molly.

"Precisely, my love," said Mr. Brougham, tightening his clasp on her hands.

"You're so clever," said Lady Molly, lost in admiration.

Once again Mrs. Townley and Lord St. Omar tried to leave the room, but this time they were forestalled by Tony Laverham's unceremonious entrance.

"Lady Molly! Where is my sword? No one can find it! And the Contessa says you must come to the sewing room immediately for a fitting!"

Lady Molly, blushing furiously, pulled her hands away from Mr. Brougham.

"Your sword is behind the sofa in the green room, I think, Mr. Laverham. And, Phoebe, how could we forget about the costumes? Both Mr. Brougham and I will have to have them altered!"

"How lucky the Contessa remembered!" said Mrs. Townley. "She's right, you know: there's no time to be lost."

Lady Molly left the room quickly, turning to give a parting smile to Mr. Brougham. The estrangement between them was over; she was delighted at the discovery that he wrote the wittiest plays since Sheridan; and she was sure all would be well as soon as they had a moment alone together. She might not have obeyed the Contessa's command so promptly had she known that it would be more than twenty-four hours before she could speak to Mr. Brougham alone.

Seekings Castle was in an uproar. Servants scurried about, rearranging potted palms, hammering together backdrops, and preparing rooms for the additional guests (such of the play's audience as chose to spend the night, their servants, and the hired orchestra for the ball) that Seekings would house. Many of the new guests had already arrived, and none of them spent more than ten minutes in the castle before learning of Lady Rich's spectacular abduction of her sister's *fiancé*. Lady Molly, as the hostess, was shielded from direct questions, and few even dared hint at what had occurred. Lady Molly treated all such references with disdainful silence, made easier by her preoccupation with *The Procrastinator* and its author.

Mr. Brougham was not so fortunate. No one had any scruples about discussing Lady Rich's flight in front of him, and in consequence he passed a disagreeable evening. When the gentlemen were left alone to drink their port after dinner, the Duke of Chettam was at the end of the table. His daughter's infidelity could not be openly discussed, but Mr. Brougham had the misfortune to be seated next to Mr. Creevey. Mr. Creevey's trip down from London had already been rewarded by the news of Lady Rich's flight, for he loved nothing so much as gossip. He referred to Lady Rich's chequered past several times, driving Mr. Brougham to drink far more than was good for him. But it was not until Mr. Creevey commented, *à propos* of nothing, that he remembered how much in love Lady

Molly had been with Sir Marius that spring almost five years before that Mr. Brougham deigned to reply.

"Why, you've been just waiting to say that, haven't you, Creevey?" Mr. Brougham said carefully, enunciating each word with precision.

The Duke, who missed nothing that passed at his dinner table, gestured to Lord St. Omar to intervene. Lord St. Omar, seated directly opposite Creevey, leaned across the table. "Easy now, Brougham," he said. "Creevey didn't mean anything by his observation."

Mr. Creevey had an acid tongue, but he never meant to offend seriously any member of the aristocracy. "No, of course I didn't mean anything, not a thing," he twittered in response to Lord St. Omar's minatory glance.

"You're her brother. Why are you taking it in such good part?" Mr. Brougham demanded of Lord St. Omar.

"Because it's the truth," Lord St. Omar said in a low voice. "But that was dogs-years ago. Everyone who's been here this winter knows Juliana was welcome to him for all of her."

"That's true," Mr. Brougham said thickly. "That's very true. Anyone could see she didn't care for Sir Marius. Couldn't they?"

"Yes, everyone in London knew that," piped Mr. Creevey, considerably illuminated by this exchange.

"There, you hear that?" said Lord St. Omar. "My sister doesn't care a whit for Sir Marius. Permit me to observe, Mr. Brougham, that you are chased."

Mr. Brougham blinked and looked round the table before he could locate the decanter at his elbow. He poured himself a generous splash. Passing the decanter to Mr. Creevey, a thought occurred to him.

"Your *younger* sister," he said.

"Yes, I speak of the younger," said Lord St. Omar. "Tell us, Mr. Creevey, is it true that the King is in ill health? We are all abuzz here at Seekings, but no one seems to know the truth."

Mr. Brougham relapsed into silence while Mr. Creevey, flattered at being thus singled out, responded at some length to Lord St. Omar's enquiry. But, however flattered, Mr. Creevey was shrewd and never forgot a piece of gossip. He filed away Mr. Brougham's agitation in his capacious memory. He passed along this knowledge to such good effect in the following weeks that Lady Molly was occasionally to find herself cut dead by ladies who held that the entire Drayton scandal was her fault.

Chapter Seventeen

Lady Molly's first thought on waking the next morning, Christmas Eve, was how glad she was that the Prince Regent had declined his invitation to attend that evening's festivities. Her responsibilities were heavy enough without the royal presence. Impelled by sheer nervousness, she jumped out of bed, dressed rapidly, and, without even ringing for a cup of coffee, ran down to the lesser ballroom to see if all was in order.

The chairs were set up just as she wanted them; the makeshift stage looked beautiful with the furniture and the backdrop Mrs. Townley had designed; the chandelier had been unveiled and dusted so that each great crystal scintillated; even Lady Molly could find nothing more to be done. On her way to the breakfast room, she encountered Mrs. Townley, who informed her that she had no time to eat. Mrs. Townley bore her off to the sewing room, where the maidservant who had stayed up late the night before to alter Lady Rich's costume was waiting.

The gown now fitted Lady Molly perfectly. She had seen it before, of course, on Lady Rich, but nevertheless Lady Molly gasped in amazement when she looked at herself in the glass. Chosen to suit Lady Rich, and the character Lady Rich was to play, the gown was more frivolous than anything Lady Molly ever wore. The satin, an exquisite shade of dusty rose, was cut closer than was the prevailing mode, and the bodice was so low that Lady Molly had to restrain an impulse to wrap a shawl round her shoulders. It was a simple gown, cut with elegant economy of line.

"I *do* look nice," Lady Molly said to Mrs. Townley, turning back from the mirror. "Like an actress, but I suppose that's the idea."

"You look better than Juliana ever did," said Mrs. Townley. "And no actress could afford so dear a gown. And most actresses would spoil it with too many trimmings."

At that moment Lord St. Omar rapped on the door. "I say, Mrs. Townley, are you done yet?" he called through it.

"Yes, just now. Do come in and see your sister!"

Lord St. Omar entered, Mr. Brougham behind him.

"Molly, you look lovely," her brother said. "Your hair's not arranged, of course. But the gown suits you."

"I thought she might wear her hair down," said Mrs. Townley. "Arabella's young, after all. Her hair's so pretty, and Molly'll never have another chance to wear her hair loose in public."

Lady Molly had been caught by the gentlemen's entrance in an attempt to push her hair to one side. She stood still, one hand still entangled in a curl, waiting for Mr. Brougham's opinion.

"God, you are beautiful," Mr. Brougham said softly after a moment.

Lord St. Omar and Mrs. Townley tactfully ignored this remark, but the servants whispered in the corner.

"What do you think, Molly?" asked Mrs. Townley. "Should your hair be left loose?"

"Yes. Without question," said Mr. Brougham.

No one said anything for a few minutes, then Mrs. Townley realised that they were wasting time.

"Now go away again so Molly can change," she said. "We'll be out shortly. Then you can try on your costume, Mr. Brougham."

Lord St. Omar and Mr. Brougham obediently disappeared. Lady Molly slipped off the rose-coloured dress, her hands caressing the fine satin. She put back on her old blue kerseymere frock, thanked the servant, and she and Mrs. Townley left the room. They passed the two gentlemen in the hallway.

"Now practise your lines, Molly!" exhorted Lord St. Omar.

Mr. Brougham put a hand on her arm as she passed him. "I'll talk to you tonight?"

"Yes, I'll talk to you tonight," Lady Molly promised.

The rest of Christmas Eve passed before Lady Molly could think. She had a hundred things to do: deciding the proper seating at the dinner table, the amount of champagne that should be put on ice for the ball, whether the supper should be at one or two, how many waltzes the orchestra should play, and all the other myriad arrangements for the ball. Lady Molly's thoughts were tangled. She made her decisions absently and ran through her lines with Mrs. Townley (they all having decided that an actual rehearsal on the day of the performance would be too exhausting) with no emotion in her voice.

Visions ran through her mind: Sir Marius kissing Lady Rich during rehearsals; Mr. Brougham kissing her in the darkened gallery; Lady Rich biting into a chocolate as she suggested putting on a play by Templeton Blaine; Major Costigan assuring her that Mr. Blaine was a reclusive fellow; and, recurrently, Mr. Brougham leaning against the wall in Lady Rich's drawing room and telling her as if it were the merest commonplace that he wanted to marry her.

Mrs. Townley saw that Lady Molly's mind was elsewhere. She had no doubt as to what Molly was thinking of. Romance hadn't seemed to impair Mr. Brougham's acting ability, Mrs. Townley reflected tartly. At least Lady Molly was word-perfect in her part; Mrs. Townley could only hope that she would wake from her dream in time to act with some feeling.

Lady Molly's abstraction continued through dinner, to which she was escorted by the Duke of Rutland. An amiable gentleman, the Duke did not seem to mind his hostess's vague answers and inattention, but Mrs. Townley, watching from her less exalted seat far down the table, was dismayed.

She need not have worried. Lady Molly's abstraction vanished the moment she put on the rose-coloured dress. She consented to have a little rouge rubbed on her cheeks but refused to have her eyelids darkened. Then the elder Miss Fancot (whose piano playing was better than her singing) began to play the lilting tune that served as an overture. Lady Molly kissed Mrs. Townley and thanked her for her efforts of the last two days. Then Lady Molly strolled out of the rose saloon and onto the stage, determined to do her best for the play.

Lord St. Omar stood beside Mrs. Townley in preparation for their entrance.

"It will work," he said to her with conviction.

"I beg your pardon?"

"Molly. And Mr. Brougham. They'll do well."

"I feel as if I've dressed a wooden puppet and thrust it on the stage. You truly think she'll do well?"

"Just listen," hissed Lord St. Omar, with a gesture towards the stage.

Lady Molly's voice, firm and sure, spoke Arabella's opening lines. For the first time, she spoke them with conviction. As befitted the part, Lady Molly sounded young, carefree, and adorable.

"Good heavens," said Mrs. Townley. "She was so stilted during rehearsals."

"We're lucky Brougham's playing the hero," said Lord St. Omar. "I'm sure that's what's brought her to life. Isn't that our cue?"

He and Mrs. Townley left the rose saloon and walked out onto the stage.

As always, Templeton Blaine enthralled the audience. Lady Molly was vivacious and clever; Mrs. Townley rivalled her charm; Lord St. Omar splendidly portrayed a society popinjay; Tony Laverham could draw a laugh with a single gesture, so impeccable was his comic timing. But all this mattered little to the audience who heard *The Procrastinator* for the first time. They would have laughed if the script had been read aloud by a Methodist minister. *The Procrastinator* was Templeton Blaine at his finest, and the *ton* knew no finer playwright.

Mr. Brougham, waiting in the wings for his entrance, was warmed by their applause and laughter. He had been too preoccupied to remember the joy of opening night, a joy that was never unmixed with terror that he might have lost his gift. Each time, that terror had passed and he had revelled in the delight he had brought to his audience. This time, his pleasure was more poignant than ever, because he knew the audience. He could look through the curtains rigged up at the back of the stage and see old Lady Wellburn wheezing with laughter over one of his general's absurdities, or the Duke of Chettam leaning forward so as not to miss a word of dialogue. Mr. Brougham listened to Lady Molly trip delightfully through her silliest speech and remembered, with a curious shiver, that the next scene, his entrance, was concerned primarily with his attempt to steal a kiss from Arabella. Invigorated by the storm of clapping that followed Tony Laverham's exit, Mr. Brougham sauntered onto the stage and proceeded to shock and delight the audience with the most convincing display of passion they had seen on any stage.

The Duke of Chettam leaned back in his chair, highly amused by Mr. Brougham's courtship of his daughter. Lady Amelia, who had been persuaded to leave her bedchamber to see the play, sat bolt upright, her face expressing profound horror. The audience buzzed during the intermission: not only was the play delicious, the music exquisite, and the acting amazingly lifelike, but Lady Molly Drayton was revealed to have found a quick replacement for her errant betrothed. Mr. Creevey chuckled to himself. Lord St. Omar and Mrs. Townley, well pleased, grinned at each other in silent triumph. Sincerity rang in Mr. Brougham's tones. He and Lady Molly were far more sympathetic lovers than Sir Marius and Lady Rich.

A more experienced actress might have dared remonstrate with Mr. Brougham for the licence he took that evening, but Lady Molly was unable to discourage him. She merely succumbed to the pleasure of her *rôle*, blissfully embracing Mr. Brougham, sure that she, like Arabella, was destined to live happily ever after. She didn't care about the three hundred people watching them, and she knew that Mr. Brougham had forgiven her for their quarrel. Clasping his hand as they bowed to the audience at the end of the play, Lady Molly had only time to whisper to him, "They love it!" before a horde of well-wishers descended.

Lady Molly and Mr. Brougham were swept apart in the storm of congratulations. She glimpsed his dark head across the room, but she knew that any effort to speak to him now would be wasted. It was late, but the evening was not yet over. The servants began to shepherd the guests across the great hall to the grand ballroom, which was never opened more than once a year. There the guests could obtain champagne or orgeat; the actors, still in costume, mingled with their audience; the orchestra struck up a merry tune by Templeton Blaine.

"What a charming conceit!" Lady Molly exclaimed as she entered the grand ballroom and discerned the melody. "Whose idea was that?"

"Father's, of course," said Lord St. Omar, who was at her elbow. "Come, let's dance, Molly. You must feel light as a bird! Aren't you glad it's over?"

Lady Molly did feel lighthearted. After one vain look round the crowded room for Mr. Brougham, she permitted her brother to lead her onto the floor.

Mr. Brougham was less reticent than Lady Molly. He saw Mrs. Townley by the entrance to the ballroom and made his way to her side.

"Where is Lady Molly?" he asked her. "Is she dancing?"

Mrs. Townley was unable to help him, but pointed out that Lady Molly's rose-colored dress should be easy to identify.

"I'd know her in a crowd ten times this size," said Mr. Brougham. He bowed to Mrs. Townley and walked off to look for his beloved. He spotted her just before her dance with Lord St. Omar ended. He was at her side when the music stopped.

"May I have this dance, Lady Molly?"

He didn't wait for her answer before taking her in his arms and whirling her away in a waltz.

"I have to talk to you," he said, so solemnly that Lady Molly missed a step. Then she looked up at his face and was reassured.

"And I to you," she said. "I'm so sorry, Kit. I was wrong, and you were right. About Juliana, I mean."

His arms tightened round her, but he didn't speak.

"What did you want to say to me?" asked Lady Molly.

"I thought we really ought to become properly betrothed this evening, after that performance."

"Your performance, you mean," said Lady Molly.

"I do?"

Lady Molly reddened and then nestled closer in his arms. "You do make me declarations in the most public places," she observed.

"It's a bad habit," said Mr. Brougham. "It means I can't kiss you."

They had waltzed close to one of the side doors by this point.

"We could leave," said Lady Molly. "Out that door."

Mr. Brougham gave a low laugh. "How shocking! But no one will be surprised."

"Then let's do it."

"Can we go for a walk in the gardens?"

"You *are* absurd," said Lady Molly.

They slipped out the side door and through several antechambers before they found themselves back in the great hall. From there they entered the lesser ballroom, empty and dark as it had been the first time they had seen it (the Duke having declared that no tidying up could be done until after Christmas Day). They walked to the far end of the vast chamber, this time Mr. Brougham leading Lady Molly. They went to the French windows overlooking the terrace. After fumbling with the lock, Mr. Brougham pushed open one window. He and Lady Molly stepped through into the chill, moonlit night.

Several minutes later, Lady Molly looked up at Mr. Brougham. "Father will be pleased," she said. "He likes you. And I shouldn't think he'll be too surprised."

"No, I shouldn't think so. Molly, my love, I asked his permission to marry you weeks ago."

"You couldn't have, not while I was still betrothed!"

"Let's say I made my sentiments clear. I don't think your father had much faith in that betrothal by that time, anyway."

"You never told me you'd spoken to Father. But then you've been very secretive, haven't you? Why didn't you tell me you were Templeton Blaine?"

"I wanted to wait till the play was over," explained Mr. Brougham. "I thought you might be angry with me for deceiving you."

"Angry with you! For writing the best play since Sheridan! I'm so proud of you."

Lady Molly kissed Mr. Brougham. Then she put a hand against his cheek and said, "It's very cold. Kit, we ought to go in."

Mr. Brougham kissed her hand. "Yes, we must. Listen, the bells are ringing. It's midnight. Christmas Day."

"A lovely time for Father to announce our engagement," said Lady Molly. "Supper's at one. He can tell everyone and they'll all toast our happiness."

They had moved no more than three paces towards the window when Mr. Brougham kissed her again. A light snow had begun to fall. The bells had stopped ringing, but another waltz tune by Templeton Blaine lilted through the night air.

ROMANCE...ADVENTURE ...DANGER...
by Best-selling author, Aola Vandergriff

You'll want to read these other *Valerie Sherwood* bestsellers . . .

_HER SHINING SPLENDOR
by Valerie Sherwood   (D30-536, $3.95)

Lenore and Lorena: their names are so alike, yet their beauties so dissimilar. Yet each is bound to reap the rewards and troubles of love. Here are the adventures of the exquisite Lenore and her beauteous daughter Lorena, each setting out upon her own odyssey of love, adventure, and fame.

_THIS TOWERING PASSION
by Valerie Sherwood   (D33-042, $2.95)

They called her "Angel" when she rode bareback into the midst of battle to find her lover. They called her "Mistress Daunt" when she lived with Geoffrey in Oxford, though she wore no ring on her finger. Wherever she traveled men called her Beauty. Her name was Lenore—and she answered only to "Love."

_THESE GOLDEN PLEASURES
by Valerie Sherwood   (D33-116, $2.95)

She was beautiful—and notorious and they called her "That Barrington Woman." But beneath the silks and the diamonds, within the supple body so many men had embraced, was the heart of a girl who yearned still for love. At fifteen she had learned her beauty was both a charm and a curse. It had sent her fleeing from Kansas, had been her downfall in Baltimore and Georgia, yet had kept her alive in the Klondike and the South Seas.

_THIS LOVING TORMENT
by Valerie Sherwood   (D30-724, $3.95)

Perhaps she was *too beautiful!* Perhaps the brawling colonies would have been safer for a plainer girl, one more demure and less accomplished in language and manner. But Charity Woodstock was gloriously beautiful with pale gold hair and topaz eyes—and she was headed for trouble. She was accused of withcraft by the man who had attacked her. She was whisked from pirate ship to plantation. Beauty might have been her downfall, but Charity Woodstock had a reckless passion to live and would challenge this new world—and win.

You'll also want to read these thrilling bestsellers by *Jennifer Wilde*...